JENNIFER BLECHER

CAMP FAMOUS

★ GREENWILLOW BOOKS ★

AN IMPRINT OF HARPERCOLLINS PUBLISHERS

Camp Famous
Text copyright © 2022 by Jennifer Blecher

www.harpercollinschildrens.com

The text of this book is set in Bookman Old Style.
Book design by Sylvie Le Floc'h

Library of Congress Cataloging-in-Publication Data

Names: Blecher, Jennifer, author.
Title: Camp Famous / Jennifer Blecher.
Description: First edition. | New York : Greenwillow Books, an Imprint of HarperCollins Publishers, [2022] | Audience: Ages 8–12. | Audience: Grades 4–6. | Summary: When eleven-year-old Abby learns she will be attending summer camp, she is excited at the idea of a fresh start, but when she discovers she is going to Camp Famous, a place exclusively for famous kids like pop stars, princesses, and geniuses, her enthusiasm turns to apprehension.
Identifiers: LCCN 2021055300 (print) | LCCN 2021055301 (ebook) | ISBN 9780063140684 (hardcover) | ISBN 9780063140707 (ebook)
Subjects: CYAC: Camps—Fiction. | Celebrities—Fiction. | Friendship—Fiction.
Classification: LCC PZ7.B61658 Cam 2022 (print) | LCC PZ7.B61658 (ebook) | DDC [Fic]—dc23
LC record available at https://lccn.loc.gov/2021055300
LC ebook record available at https://lccn.loc.gov/2021055301

22 23 24 25 26 PC/LSCH 10 9 8 7 6 5 4 3 2 1

First Edition

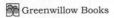 Greenwillow Books

To my mom and dad,
Pamela and Jack Ende

A cartwheel on a warm, sunny day should feel entirely happy. Especially if it's not just one cartwheel, but a whole series of cartwheels done by a whole group of girls who have just been let out of the classroom for recess. Hands land on freshly mown grass and laughter bubbles across the field, so joyful that it sounds like it's filled with glitter.

My cartwheel was not that kind of cartwheel.

Or maybe I just wasn't that kind of girl.

It was April. Teachers had started calling us "almost middle schoolers," even though there were still two months left of fifth grade. Sometimes they meant it as a compliment. Other times as a warning to improve our behavior.

No matter what, it always made me worry. How was I supposed to handle what came next when what was right in front of me kept getting trickier and trickier?

Like recess. It used to be games of tag and racing to the swings and four square tournaments. A swirl of motion. Coats tossed to the ground no matter the weather. Now everyone except me seemed to have a spot, a group, someone waiting to restart a conversation that had been cut short when the morning bell rang.

I couldn't ignore the growing suspicion that I was falling behind. That I was being forgotten.

So when Marin, the most popular girl in my class who was also actually nice, yelled, "Cartwheel contest!" I looked in the direction of her voice.

Marin and I weren't really friends, but sometimes if she liked the cover of a book I was reading, she asked to borrow it when I finished. She always returned the book with no creased pages and, if she loved the story, she hugged the book before giving it back. I liked that about her.

So even though I wasn't part of Marin's group, I followed her over to the field. The cartwheels made it easy. I could slip in without having to wait for the other girls to notice me. Or worse, ask permission to join.

I got lost in the rotation of arm, arm, foot, foot. I fell in a dizzy heap, caught my breath, and started again. It was laughter and light and freedom and . . . "Um, Abby?" said Quinn, Marin's best friend who was not nice at all.

I stopped, my arms a few degrees ahead of my body.

Quinn stood beside me. Even though my vision was blurred, the smirk on Quinn's face made it obvious that something embarrassing had happened.

And that it had happened to me.

"Maybe you should tuck your shirt in?" said Marin, pointing to her waist where her shirt was tucked into her leggings.

"Or at least wear a bra," said Quinn.

In an instant the field came into focus. Everyone else was cartwheeling with their shirts tucked into their waistbands. How had I missed that? Had everyone seen my chest? How could I be so clueless?

Laughter came from all sides. But fingers pointed in only one direction.

"Wake up, Abby," said Quinn, rolling her eyes.

But I *was* awake. I paid attention to everything. The way Quinn paused between cartwheels to throw her ponytail into a bun, twisting her hair before wrapping it tight. How Marin drank from her water bottle, examining the metallic rim to make sure that her lips landed in the exact same spot as the light pink gloss marks left from an earlier sip. How when Riley and Jayda cartwheeled right into each other, they collapsed into a happy heap instead of getting upset.

Paying attention to other people was what I did best. Most of the time.

Ms. McIntyre appeared at my side. She was the kind of teacher who could sense what was happening even if she didn't know the details.

"Abby," she said, bending down to whisper in my ear. "You okay?"

I nodded, squeezing every muscle in my face to hold back tears.

Ms. McIntyre smelled like roses and sunshine. Her eyes glowed with kindness. She placed her palm on my back and rubbed tiny circles.

I wanted to lean in and to pull away at the same time.

To start over and never, ever try again.

The recess bell rang. Ms. McIntyre hung back with me while everyone else walked ahead. I thought I could keep the tears inside. I really did. But then Quinn raised her cupped hand to Marin's ear to whisper something. Quinn glanced back at me before repeating the motion with Riley.

Quinn's gaze was a laser that shot straight into me. Once the tears started, I couldn't stop them. I stood at the edge of the field crying into the arms of my favorite teacher while everyone else in my class walked back into school.

That night a note from Ms. McIntyre was paper-clipped to the back of my vocab quiz.

Abby,

I know you had a hard day. If you could see my journal from when I was your age, the pages are filled with so many hard days. Sometimes I read what I wrote and wonder how I survived fifth grade. But I did survive. And you will, too.

I'm always here if you want to talk some more.

Sincerely,
Ms. McIntyre

I could not imagine Ms. McIntyre ever feeling the hot sting of embarrassment that I felt at recess that day. But I could imagine her writing in a journal.

Ms. McIntyre swooned when talking about a book that she couldn't wait for our class to read. She did a funny celebration dance on library day. And sometimes, when I wrote something she liked in my weekly reflection, she drew a tiny pencil heart in the margins, both sides equal and round with a perfectly crisp point at the bottom.

I reread the note. *If you could see my journal.*

I tried to picture Ms. McIntyre's journal. Maybe it had a bouquet of flowers on the cover? Maybe she wrote in pink ink? Or alternating colors? Did they even have colored ink back then?

The more I tried to imagine what Ms. McIntyre's

journal might have looked like, the more I thought about the notebook that Grandma had given me a few weeks before for my eleventh birthday. She'd slid it across the kitchen table in her apartment at the retirement village in Florida. I'd flown down all by myself from New York to spend the weekend.

"For you," Grandma had said, keeping both hands on the gift. She had an intense stare, a steadiness in her eyes. Like she was not only looking at me, but looking into me.

I lifted the present into my lap, grateful to have something to focus on other than her face.

Sometimes Grandma's gaze made confetti bombs of excitement explode in my belly. A sparkle in her eyes signaled that she saw the whole of me and loved me just the way I was. Other times that same look made me want to curl in a ball and roll away down a giant hill because Grandma seemed to be searching for something to pull out from deep inside of me.

This was one of those other times. I didn't know

what Grandma was searching for, but I guessed that it had something to do with the present.

I unwrapped the silver paper to find a fuzzy green notebook with an *A* for "Abby" in hot pink sequins. The pages were lined and tinted a pale blue.

"For you to write in," said Grandma.

"What should I write? Stories?"

"Maybe stories. Or you could write about what you're feeling. I know there's a lot going on in your head, Abby. Sometimes it helps to put your thoughts down on paper."

I flipped through the pages one more time and closed the notebook.

How could I describe that I was happy to be spending my birthday with Grandma, but also wondered if my parents had planned the trip to save me from having to host a birthday party? The worry over who would come. If anyone actually wanted to be there. What activity we should do.

How could I explain that even as I rubbed the

soft green fuzz and flipped the hot pink sequins, I also wanted to hide the notebook away in the darkness of my duffel bag because I didn't have anything worth writing?

I stood up to give Grandma a hug. As I rested my cheek against her shoulder, she squeezed me tight and whispered, "You're going to figure it out, Abby. I promise."

Grandma sounded so certain, like it was only a matter of days before the pages of the notebook would be stuffed full of entries about sleepovers, movie nights with endless candy, and trips to the mall to pick out scented bath bombs with my huge group of friends.

As if I could snap my fingers and make those sort of plans happen, which obviously I could not.

I didn't write in the notebook that night. Or the next.

When I got home from Grandma's, I slid the notebook into the top drawer of my dresser. I'd taken it out a few times since then and admired the cover, but the only thing I'd written was my full name—Abigail Jane Herman—on the very first page.

Now I walked to the dresser and pulled the notebook out carefully, as if maybe it had turned into a green dragon with hot pink scales. But the notebook was the same as when I'd left it weeks ago.

No flames. No fangs. Just empty lined pages.

I brought it to my desk and reached for my favorite pen, which was topped with a purple fluff ball. I ran the fluff against my lips.

Grandma wanted me to write about myself. Ms. McIntyre had written about herself when she was my age.

They were two of my favorite people. Maybe it was time to give it a try.

~~Dear Notebook,~~

~~Dear Journal,~~

~~Dear Diary,~~

How do I start this? Do I give you a name? You're green and pink and sparkly. So maybe I'll name you . . . Poppy? Pippa?

~~Dear Pippa,~~

No. You've got an A on your cover, which obviously stands for "Abby." But even though I'm supposed to write about my own feelings, I don't want to fill you up with all the things that I'd rather forget. You're too happy looking for that.

So how about I just call you Notebook, and I can tell you about everyone else. My notebook of observations. Like my science journal. But for life.

So here it goes, Notebook. Wish me luck!

Never forget that before you do a cartwheel you have to tuck in your shirt. This is something that is so obvious no one says it out loud. You're just supposed to know it. And if you don't know it, someone like Quinn will remind you in front of everyone.

In case that makes Quinn sound nice, you should know that she is not nice. You can practically see her celebrate when someone else makes a mistake. Like other people's embarrassment is her favorite flavor of milkshake, and she wants to drink it up with a striped straw.

Why do people like Quinn have so many friends? Why is Marin (who is actually nice) best friends with someone like Quinn?

Is it because when Quinn's chasing down a ball in PE she looks like she's gliding instead of running? Or because Quinn's allowed to watch whatever she wants on TV and then she says the character names like they're actual people who you're supposed to know even when you've never heard of them? Or is it the way she paints her nails in alternating glitter colors and they always look so smooth—not lumpy or chipped.

Why doesn't Quinn's nail polish chip??!!

I guess what I really want to know is: Why does being Quinn work for making friends? And why does being me not work?

Sorry, Notebook. I just meant to tell you the rule about cartwheels. The other stuff slipped out. I'll do better next time.

Love,
Abby

The next morning I packed my backpack with all the normal school things: math workbook, science binder, language arts binder, water bottle, and a book to read at silent reading (and also probably recess).

I almost left my notebook on my desk, but the hot pink sequins sparkled in the morning light like they were dying to come along.

I had no choice. I couldn't resist sequins.

When I walked into the kitchen, Mom noticed the notebook right away. "Is that the one Grandma got you for your birthday?"

I nodded, wishing I had it in my backpack instead of carrying it in my hand. What I had written last night was private. I didn't want Mom to get curious.

While Mom spread peanut butter over toast, I slipped the notebook into my backpack and zipped it closed.

Mom was a housing rights lawyer who argued cases in court. If she read what I wrote, she would shake her head and list all the reasons why I should not be comparing myself to other girls, especially not girls who watched inappropriate TV shows.

Every single word would sound smart and be true.

But even when Mom's words made sense in my brain, they didn't always make sense in my heart. Whenever I tried to explain to Mom that I was lonely, that I didn't understand why it was so hard for me to make friends, she would immediately suggest some new after-school activity. Maybe tennis lessons at the public courts next to the library? Or pottery at the community center? How about theater?

Mom's answer to every problem was doing more. Like if I was busy enough, I would forget that I had signed up for the activity alone. Which was ironic because Mom refused to let me do the one thing that I wanted most: go to sleepover camp at Camp Longatocket.

My old babysitter, Juliet, had gone to Camp Longatocket. She used to tell me about it, her voice going all soft, like she was wrapped up in a snuggly blanket.

Camp Longatocket was Juliet's favorite place in the world.

Juliet was away at college now, but I'd been on the Camp Longatocket website a million times and memorized all the pictures. There was a lake that sparkled in the sun. Cabins with rocking chairs on the front porches. Smiling girls with their arms wrapped around one another. Hand-painted signs nailed to trees.

I wanted to meet those girls. Swim in that lake. See where those signs pointed.

Also, there was part of me that wondered if I was so lonely because my person, the one who couldn't wait to continue our conversation as soon as Ms. McIntyre let us out for recess, just wasn't at my school.

Maybe there was nothing wrong with me except bad friendship luck.

Would someone at Camp Longatocket like me just the way I was? If I went, would I finally find out how it feels to have a best friend?

I would never know. Mom and Dad said sleepover camp was too expensive. Too far away. They'd miss me too much.

So after months of begging, I'd finally given up asking.

Besides, according to the website, Camp Longatocket was already full for the summer.

I poured a bowl of cereal while Mom finished her toast. Then Dad walked into the kitchen wearing real clothes, and I froze mid-bite.

Dad worked from home writing articles for nature magazines. He only wore pants with zippers and shirts with collars when he had a meeting or an appointment. And he *always* made a big deal about that the night before, complaining about the hassle of buttons and belts. He hadn't said anything at dinner last night.

"Why are you wearing those clothes?" I asked.

Dad glanced at Mom as he poured a cup of coffee. "You didn't tell her?"

"I was waiting for you."

"Tell me what?"

I hated when Mom and Dad talked over my head. It was like getting to the end of a mystery novel where all the questions were about to be answered, but you still had pages to go before finding out the true villain.

I repeated the question.

Mom slid onto the stool next to mine. "Ms. McIntyre emailed us last night. She asked if we could come in to speak with her in person. I'm in court starting tomorrow, so this was the only time I could make it work."

"Ms. McIntyre wants you to come into school? Why?"

"We were hoping you might know," said Mom. "Did something happen?"

I shook my head, even though crying on the playground definitely counted as *something*. But Ms. McIntyre had promised that it wasn't my fault. She'd said it over and over. "It's not your fault, Abby. You didn't do anything wrong."

If I hadn't done anything wrong, then why had she called my parents in for a meeting?

"Well, we'll find out soon enough," said Mom. "Let's get going. You don't have to take the bus today, Abby. We can all drive together."

We got to school before the main doors were even unlocked. Ms. McIntyre was waiting to let us in. I tried to catch her eye, but she just smiled like it was any old day. Any old parent-teacher conference.

I waited outside the classroom while my parents met with Ms. McIntyre. The time tick-tocked super slow. With each passing minute, more people entered the building until the hallway was full, my entire class waiting outside the closed door.

I wanted to tear a page from my notebook, print "YOU HAVE TO LEAVE RIGHT NOW!!" in large letters, and slide it under the classroom door.

When that door opened and my parents walked out in front of everyone, it was going to be a giant, humiliating disaster. For the second day in a row.

Everyone in my class would be thinking the same thing: *Why are Abby's parents here? What did she do wrong?*

Even I didn't know the answer to that.

"What's taking so long?" whined Quinn, her arms crossed. "Ms. McIntyre always opens the door by now."

"No idea," said Marin.

"Oh, well," said Quinn. "At least we can talk about K.C."

Marin brought her hands to her heart and sighed. "K.C." She said the letters slowly, as if they were floating in the air surrounded by heart emojis.

Who was K.C.? I scanned through the class list in my mind. There was no one with those initials. Then Quinn began to sing a song about beach rocks, and I realized that K.C. stood for Kai Carter, a super-popular singer who always wore a red hoodie. Kai Carter was so cute that he made chewing on the ends of his sweatshirt's drawstrings look delicious, not disgusting.

"I know Kai Carter," said Oliver Frank.

Oliver was a super-smart boy in my class. His hair flopped down to the edge of his glasses, and he had a habit of tucking his chin into the collar of his shirt, so it was easy to overlook him. Or even forget he was standing right there. Until, like now, Oliver popped into a conversation with no warning, as if the entire topic had been his idea.

"Duh," said Quinn, rolling her eyes. "*Everyone* knows Kai Carter. He's like the most popular singer in the world right now. I've memorized his entire new album."

"Me too," said Marin.

I made a mental note to write in my notebook about memorizing Kai Carter. Had I heard his new album? Or just his old one? How was I supposed to know which was which?

Oliver Frank raised his pointer finger in an attempt to say more, but at that same moment the classroom door swung open. My parents stepped out. Together. With Ms. McIntyre right behind them.

"Oh, hello, Mr. and Ms. Herman," said Oliver, as if he was welcoming my parents to his hallway.

"Uh, hello, Oliver," said Dad.

I wanted Oliver to be his most Oliver-ish and start a random conversation with Dad so I could slip into the classroom behind my parents, unnoticed.

At the same time, I wanted to pull Mom and Dad aside so they could tell me what Ms. McIntyre had said. Mom had a concerned expression, and a strand of hair was loose from her normally perfect bun. But Dad smiled and gave me a thumbs-up, as if he'd had a completely different conversation than Mom.

Before I could learn more, the hallway came to life. Shoulders bumped into mine. Sneakers shuffled along the floor. Murmured greetings of "Good morning, Ms. McIntyre. Good morning, Ms. McIntyre. Good morning, Ms. McIntyre," drifted into the air.

I'd done the same routine every school day since kindergarten—waited in line, made eye contact with my teacher, said my morning greeting. So even though my mind was on my parents and the mysterious meeting, my body moved automatically.

I entered the classroom and sat down at my desk, only looking up when Marin said, "Hey, Abby. I hope everything's okay. Do you want an eraser? I have a whole bunch."

Marin opened her clenched hand to reveal a bunch of mini-animal erasers. The kind that are way cuter than they are effective. I picked out a tiny pink pig.

"Thanks," I said. I steadied the pig on the corner of my desk. His cheeks were as round as apples. His tail curled in tight curlicue twists.

He was only an eraser, but he helped.

I had just decided to name him Wilbur, after *Charlotte's Web*, when the edge of a backpack knocked him off my desk and onto the floor. Wilbur landed belly up, his four pig legs in the air.

"Oops," said Quinn. "My bad. Are you going to go cry about it to Ms. McIntyre and get me in trouble?"

What? Did Quinn think that my parents had asked for a meeting with Ms. McIntyre? Because I had complained about Quinn teasing me after the cartwheel situation?

I wasn't going to cry, but I did want to throw Wilbur in Quinn's face.

How could two best friends be so different? Marin had given me a sympathy pig, and Quinn had knocked it to the ground and made me feel even worse.

I did not throw Wilbur. Instead, I placed him back on my desk. Then I leaned down to whisper into his tiny pig ear, "Sorry, Wilbur. We're going to get Quinn back someday. I promise."

Wilbur was named in honor of a talking pig, but thankfully he was just an eraser and couldn't ask me *how* we were going to get our revenge.

Because the truth was, I had no idea.

After what Quinn said, I didn't talk to Ms. McIntyre privately all day. I didn't want anyone to think I was a tattletale.

When I got home, Mom and Dad said Ms. McIntyre had only wanted to let them know how hard I was working in class and how much she enjoyed being my teacher.

In other words, they were flat-out lying. There was no way Ms. McIntyre would call a special in-person meeting just to say I was a good kid.

For days there was an extra presence in our

house. A shadowy, shifting, ghostlike suspicion that something was up. And no one was willing to fill me in.

Finally, on Sunday night, Mom and Dad knocked gently on my bedroom door.

I turned over the scrap paper where I was writing out the lyrics to Kai Carter's newest song. Marin and Quinn had already memorized his entire album. I wasn't even close and thought writing down the words might help me remember them. But no way did I want Mom and Dad seeing the lines about first kisses and broken hearts. I slid the paper into my desk drawer on top of my green notebook. Safe and hidden.

"Can we come in?" asked Mom.

"Okay," I called.

I hopped over to my bed, crossing my legs as if I had been there the whole time. Whatever Mom and Dad were going to tell me needed the softness of my fuzzy teal blanket. The closeness of my stuffed animals. Maybe a pillow or two to bury my head into if things got really bad.

My bedroom door opened. Mom and Dad were holding hands. Which was not abnormal, but also not normal. I grabbed a handful of blanket and squeezed.

"We have some news," said Mom.

"Good news?" I asked. "Or bad?"

"Good news," said Dad. "Very, very good news."

I loosened my grip on the blanket. Dad was smiling, but Mom was biting her lower lip. Not like she was holding back a smile of excitement—like she was holding back a worried exhale.

I focused on Dad. "What is it?"

Dad did a long drumroll on my desk. It was torture!

I threw my stuffed-animal walrus at him. Finally he stopped drumming and said, "You're going to sleepover camp, Abby! Actual sleepover camp with cabins and a lake and bugs that climb all over you!"

Dad flopped onto the bed and tickled me as if his fingers were spiders. I was so busy squirming and laughing and trying to escape his finger spiders that I almost couldn't take in the news.

I was going to sleepover camp? Me? Abigail Jane Herman?

The information was so surprising that the words might not have settled in my brain even if I'd been sitting perfectly still, hands folded in my lap, ankles neatly crossed.

I'd been begging and pleading (and begging a little more) for so long! How could this finally be happening?

Camp Longatocket had posted their packing list last week. They were getting ready to move the docks out of storage and check the cabins for winter rot. They'd even started the fifty-day countdown to camp. There was a ticking clock with glowing digital numbers in the top corner of the website. The same website that had announced a month ago that Camp Longatocket was full for the season.

"How did you get me a spot?"

"It was actually Ms. McIntyre's doing," said Mom.

"Ms. McIntyre? Was this what the meeting at school was about?"

Mom nodded. All this time I'd been thinking the meeting was about something bad, when it was actually about something great. A pencil heart in the margins of my weekly reflection times one thousand! A heart explosion!

But what had Ms. McIntyre said? How did she know about Camp Longatocket? Had I mentioned it in my weekly reflection?

When I asked, Mom pressed her fingers against the spot on her lip where her teeth had just been biting. "Ms. McIntyre's brother runs a sleepover camp," she explained. "She thought it might be nice for you to go this summer and meet a whole new bunch of kids. Almost like practice for starting middle school next year."

"So not Camp Longatocket?"

Dad shook his head. "Not Camp Longatocket. But this camp is the same. In many ways. Pretty much all the ways. Mostly."

"What's it called?"

"It's called . . . " Dad paused, as if trying to

remember. "It's called Camp Summerah. As in 'summer,' but with an *a-h* at the end."

"Can I see the website?"

"There's no website," said Mom. "Camp Summerah is . . . old-fashioned."

"But also modern," added Dad. "So modern that it's off-the-grid. A true digital detox kind of place."

My parents were being weird. But who cared! I was going to sleepover camp!

I leaped off the bed and ran to Mom. Clearly Mom wasn't as excited about the decision as Dad. Maybe that's why it took so long for them to tell me the news. Because they'd been arguing about whether to let me go.

So I wrapped my arms around Mom as tight as I possibly could. She placed one hand on the back of my head and gave me a long kiss. With my firm squeeze I tried to tell Mom that she'd made the right decision. She didn't need to worry.

I was going to have the best time ever.

Dear Notebook,

I am going to SLEEPOVER CAMP!!!!!

If you had a keyboard I would be typing one million smiling emoji faces and rainbows and poops with exploding heads (even though they're gross) because I am so excited!

But I'm glad you don't have a keyboard because then I wouldn't be able to take you with me. Do you want to come with me to sleepover camp? Of course you do! We're going to have so much fun at Camp Summerah!

It's kind of a weird name, but I think that's just a camp thing. Dad said it's pretty much the same as Camp Longatocket. I wish there was a website so I could look up the packing list and see pictures. What if the girls in the pictures don't look friendly? What if they look mean? What if they are mean, like Quinn?

Sorry, Notebook. I promised that I wouldn't fill you with sad things, only important life observations. But I'm nervous. Sleepover camp is my chance to make new friends. Maybe even a best friend.

What if I mess it up? What if I'm doomed?

Things always seem to go wrong. Like at school this week. I was Quinn's partner in math. That's how I found out that Marin and Quinn and Riley and Jayda had a group sleepover last night. For Quinn's math fraction word problem she wrote: "If five girls split three huge bags of gummies at their sleepover on Saturday night, what fraction of the total candy does each girl get?"

I wanted to point out that six girls splitting three bags of gummies would be much easier math. But math wasn't the point. Obviously. Before I even solved the problem, Quinn leaned over to Jayda and asked super loud if she was allowed to eat gummies with her braces. When Jayda said no, Quinn crossed out "gummies" and replaced it with "chocolate."

People like Quinn can make anything mean, even math. The sneaky part made the being left-out part feel even worse. I wish I knew why.

I really hope no one is sneaky mean at Camp Summerah. They won't be, right?

At least I'll have you with me. I'm going to pay attention to every single thing and write it all down so I don't forget. I'm not going to mess anything up. I promise.

Love,
Abby

I started getting ready for Camp Summerah right away. Mom printed the packing list from her email, and I taped it above my desk. I placed neat check marks with my purple fluff pen next to the items as I collected them: bug spray, flashlight, shower caddy, laundry bag.

The Camp Summerah packing list was almost identical to the Camp Longatocket packing list, which was a good sign. I still didn't know very much about Camp Summerah. Ms. McIntyre clearly didn't like talking about camp at school. But when no one else was nearby, she would answer some of my questions about the activities they offered, the number of girls in a cabin, the food. And whenever I thanked her for getting me a spot, she would hug me and promise that it was going be "a life-changing summer."

I was so ready for my life to change.

I stacked my piles of shirts, shorts, underwear, socks, and other clothes in the corner of my room. If I wore something to school, I removed it from the pile and then added it right back after it was washed. The neat stacks were the last thing I saw at night and the first thing I saw in the morning. They made camp feel closer. Something physical to remind me that my dream was actually coming true.

Finally, after weeks of waiting, it was time to lift my piles from the floor and place them in a large navy duffel bag. I put my notebook in my backpack next to some paperback books for the plane ride. At the last minute, I decided to bring my pig eraser, Wilbur, as well.

Wilbur reminded me of Quinn, but also of Marin. I didn't want the Quinn part of my life to come with me to camp, but I liked bringing the Marin part.

Marin was a friend magnet. When she'd opened her palm that morning at school, she wasn't just giving me a pig eraser in a pile of other animal erasers; she was giving me a sympathy hug.

Maybe I could do the same for someone at camp?

My hand shook as I dropped Wilbur into the front pocket of my backpack and zipped it closed. I wanted only to be excited, but there was so much to worry about. What if giving someone a used pig eraser was weird?

It probably was, right? Like, *super* weird.

I was about to take Wilbur out of my backpack and place him back on my desk when Dad appeared at my door. "Our ride is coming in ten minutes. You ready?"

I nodded. "Ready."

Dad and I each took a handle of the duffel bag

and carried it down the stairs. Dad groaned as he hoisted the bag next to the large suitcases already waiting on the front steps for the ride to the airport.

Mom and Dad were going on a bird-watching trip in the desert for one of Dad's magazine assignments. While I had been stacking T-shirts and shorts in my bedroom, they had been laying out camping equipment, binoculars, and matching khaki vests with loaded pockets on the dining room table.

Mom never went on assignment with Dad. But since I was going to be away at sleepover camp, she'd asked for time off from work. She'd been debating what novels to pack for weeks.

My parent's flight to the desert left a few hours after my flight to Camp Summerah, so we all went to the airport together. As we drove away from our house, Mom reached over and squeezed my hand. I squeezed back once before pulling my hand away and sliding it under my thighs.

I wanted to skip this whole part. Saying good-bye to my parents. The airplane ride to a small airport in Vermont, where a counselor would be waiting for me with a "Camp Summerah" sign that said my name.

I just wanted to be at camp already.

I looked out the car window as Mom and Dad repeated all the things that I already knew. They would be out of cell phone range, so I should call Grandma in case of emergency. They would be thinking of me the entire time and knew I was going to have an amazing experience. They trusted me to make the right decisions and always be kind.

By the time we arrived at the airport, even the driver seemed sick of hearing it.

"Well," said Dad as we unloaded our bags. "This is quite the hullabaloo."

That was Dad-talk for busy and hectic. Which it was. Photographers were standing in a tight pack outside the sliding glass doors, pointing their long-lensed cameras toward the check-in area.

"What's going on?" I asked.

Mom ignored me, but a photographer answered my question. "Camp Famous," he said. "The kids should be arriving any minute."

"What's Camp Famous?"

The photographer lowered his camera and shook his head, as if it was the dumbest question he'd ever heard. "Where the most famous kids in the world go to sleepover camp. The place is in nowheresville and strictly off-limits. No helicopter flyovers, no speedboat drive-bys, no drones. This is the last glimpse we're gonna get of the famous kids for three weeks. That means both me and my bank account need this shot. So move along."

I was confused, and also kind of offended, when suddenly the cameras started *click, click, clicking*. The noise reminded me of that unfortunate time in kindergarten when my parents forced me to take tap dance lessons. It was fast and furious, echoing off the hard surfaces of the airport.

"Come on, Abby," said Mom, grabbing me by

the elbow. "Let's check our bags and get to the gate."

I followed my parents to the airline counter, rising onto my tiptoes to peek at the famous kids. Would they look as nervous about going to Camp Famous as I felt about going to Camp Summerah? But the photographers were a human wall of backs and hunched shoulders. I couldn't see anything other than the occasional flash of light.

"Hullabaloo," said Dad, pulling me toward the security line. "Quite the hullabaloo."

Mom shot him a look. "Exactly."

We passed through security and found an empty corner near my gate. Mom sat down next to me and placed her hand on my arm. She was about to speak when the sound of the famous kids walking down the airport corridor stopped her. They were a slow, steady, graceful thump of cool.

From behind the security check-in at the end of the terminal, photographers called out their names with the desperation of people facing imminent death.

"Isabella!"

"Over here!"

"Cameron!"

"Turn around! One last wave for your fans!"

As the famous kids got closer, Mom's grip on my arm got tighter. She rose from her seat and kneeled on the ground in front of me. "Abby," she said. "I need you to listen to me."

Did she not hear the shouts? Did she not see how close the famous kids were?

I'd been listening to Mom for the entire ride to the airport. For my entire life! I knew everything she had to say. Then Dad kneeled down beside her. He placed one hand on my knee and the other on Mom's shoulder.

What was happening?

"I'm just going to spit it out," said Mom. "Abby, you're not going to Camp Summerah. You're going to Camp Famous."

If Mom *had* actually spit, if a spray of saliva had landed smack in the center of my eyeballs, I could not have been more surprised.

"What?"

"It's true," said Dad. "You're going to Camp Famous."

I was all for repetition. I'd been playing the same Kai Carter songs for weeks. But in this case, saying the words a second time did not help. Clearly my parents were losing it.

"But we already checked my bag," I said slowly.

"Right. To Camp Famous," said Dad.

"What happened to Camp Summerah?"

Had they gotten a text message or email on the way to the airport? Had Camp Summerah burned down?

"It never existed," said Dad. "I made it up. Clever, right? Like, ah, I love summer. But in reverse. Get it?"

I looked from Dad to Mom. Dad babbled when he was nervous. Mom was the opposite. Nerves focused her. That's why she was so good at arguing cases in court.

Except that Mom seemed similarly rattled, her eyes moving rapidly across my face. "We weren't entirely honest with you, Abby," she said. "But for a good reason. If we'd told you that you were going to Camp Famous, you would have started searching online and read the tabloid articles about the place. We didn't want you to get nervous about going. That's why we're surprising you." Mom hesitated. She did jazz hands. "Surprise!"

Of course I would have gotten all nervous about it! Had they heard what that photographer said? Camp Famous was where the most famous kids in the world went to sleepover camp!

I was the least famous kid in the world. I didn't have a single sports trophy on my bookshelf. Not one shiny ribbon hanging from my door handle. I'd never even had a best friend.

"But what about Ms. McIntyre's brother?" I said. "That's how I got a spot."

"Ms. McIntyre's brother runs Camp Famous," said Mom.

Mom's confession was a lollipop after a flu shot. For a second it made me feel better. But then I realized what it meant: Ms. McIntyre had been lying to me as well. All those times at recess when I'd whispered questions about sleepover camp, she'd answered as if I was going to a normal camp, not a camp for celebrities!

"But I'm not famous. . . . " I trailed off as I caught sight of two famous kids.

The first was Princess Isabella Victoria. She had the exact same look of amused boredom as she did on the cover of *People* magazine, where she'd posed on the front steps of a huge castle wearing a white ball gown and hot pink Converse sneakers. The caption underneath said: "No Glass Slippers for This Modern Princess." A vibe of I-dare-you-to-mess-with-me wafted off the magazine cover.

The second kid I recognized was Kai Carter. *Kai Carter! K.C.!* He was wearing his signature red sweatshirt and chewing on the drawstrings. His hair swooped across his forehead in one smooth wave. I looked over my shoulder for Marin and Quinn. Surely they would come racing around the corner, their arms waving, their screams piercing.

Before I could see any other famous kids clearly enough to recognize them, Mom put her hands against my cheeks. She brought her face close to mine. "Abigail, listen to me. This is what you wanted. Sleepover camp. You can do this. Dad and I will be waiting right here when you get back."

Dad kissed the top of my head. "Listen to your mother, Abby. She is very wise."

It was as if I'd been sucked into a tornado. Everything that used to be on solid ground was suddenly swirling. I wrapped my arms around my parents in a combination of excitement and fear. With my arms still locked around their backs, Mom and Dad shuffled me out of our corner spot.

Then I felt Dad lift his arm from my back as if he was waving to someone.

The very last someone I ever expected to see standing among the most famous kids in the world.

6

"Oliver?"

Oliver Frank smiled at me, nodding as he greeted my family. "Hello, Abby. Hello, Ms. Herman. Mr. Herman."

"Oh, thank goodness," said Mom. "You're here."

I was so confused that I wished for a second tornado to come and reverse spin me back to when life made sense.

Had Ms. McIntyre got Oliver a spot at Camp Famous as well?

Before I could ask, two large men with clear,

curled wires behind their ears spread their arms to encircle the famous kids and steer them toward a metal door in the corner of the terminal.

Oliver reached out to me. "Come on, Abby. Let's go."

"You're going to Camp Famous, too?"

"Yep!"

"And you're okay with that?"

"I'm more than okay," said Oliver. "I'm ecstatic. We're going to camp!"

I wanted to be ecstatic. It had been one of our vocab words at school. But a different vocab word was more accurate: *hesitant.* Extremely hesitant. I wrapped my arms around Mom. "I don't know. . . . "

"Come on now," said one of the men, widening his arms to include me and Oliver. "Move it along."

Mom put her hand on the man's thick arm. "I need one minute with my daughter."

Mom was not scary. But she could drop her voice in a way that made even burly men with earpieces shiver. The big dude stepped back.

JENNIFER BLECHER

"Abby," she said. "You can do this."

"I don't belong there. When everyone finds out, they're going to hate me."

"Abby, if those kids have any brains inside their famous heads, they are going to love you. Just be yourself. You are perfect exactly as you are."

I knew Mom loved me. She said it every single day. But I also knew there was a part of her that wanted me to be more. To sign up for the activities. Join the teams. Stand on center stage and shine.

Mom had never told me that I was perfect just the way I was before. Even though I was certain that the words weren't true, they filled me with a dose of courage. And if Oliver Frank was brave enough to go to Camp Famous, so was I.

"Okay," I said.

"That's our girl," cheered Dad.

"We love you," shouted Mom.

"This way, young lady," said the big dude. "Hurry."

Oliver and I followed the famous kids through

52

the metal door marked "Do Not Enter." I kept my eyes forward. If I turned back and saw my parents, there was a decent chance I would pull a preschool move and run crying into their arms.

On the other side of the door was a stairway that led outside. The sun was glaring, the air buzzing with the whirl of airplane engines. I'd never been on an airport runway before. Every step seemed dangerous, like walking on hot lava.

"Oliver," I said.

"Just breathe, Abby. You're almost to the plane."

If I could have chosen anyone from my class to be with at Camp Famous, it would have been Marin. But I was still grateful that Oliver was beside me. Part of me wanted to reach out and grab his hand. But I was too old, and too shaky, for that.

It had been exciting to think about going to normal sleepover camp by myself. A chance to start fresh. But going to a camp for rock stars and royalty by myself? No way.

We reached a parked plane with a set of stairs

leading up to its open door. I gripped the railings and concentrated on not falling through the open risers.

Inside the plane, tiny lights sparkled in the ceiling like stars. The side panels were trimmed in polished wood. The hardware was gold. I sank into a leather seat in the second row, scooting to the window so Oliver could sit next to me.

"How are you so calm?" I whispered to Oliver.

"I'm not calm," said Oliver, beginning to bounce in his seat. "I'm excited. See?" His bouncing picked up speed.

Over Oliver's bobbing head, I watched the kids boarding the plane. There were about twenty of them and most looked regular-ish. There was Kai Carter and Princess Isabella Victoria. A girl who looked familiar from TV and a boy wearing all black who kept his head hung low. Some kids had backpacks like mine. Others pulled small rolling suitcases.

Not one single kid appeared confused or concerned.

A boy with a paint-splattered shirt gave Oliver a high five. A girl with cascading wavy hair smiled and waved at him.

Oliver only stopped bouncing when the safety announcements started to play and he was forced to buckle his seat belt.

Suddenly we were rolling down the runway. I tried to talk to Oliver, but he kept shushing me to listen to the announcements. It was only after the plane lifted into the air that Oliver turned to me and asked, "So, are *you* excited?"

"I'm more confused than excited. What are *we* doing going to Camp Famous?"

Oliver shrugged. "Camping? With famous kids?"

"That's not what I mean, Oliver. I mean, why did Ms. McIntyre think this was a good idea? We're just regular kids."

"Don't worry, Abby. So are they."

How was Oliver so calm? We were lifting up through the clouds in the fanciest airplane I'd ever seen. I had no idea where we were headed or how long we'd be flying. Yet Oliver was strumming his fingers against the armrest like it was no big deal. He didn't even stop strumming when one of the large men with an earpiece lumbered down the aisle.

"Don't worry," said Oliver, following my eyes. "Once we land, you'll never see them again. They're just security for the trip over."

"How do you know all this?"

Oliver ballooned his cheeks like a blowfish, deflating them with a slow exhale. "I, uh, have to use the bathroom. It's an emergency. Be right back."

As Oliver slid off his leather seat, I almost grabbed his shirt. Instead I looked out the window. We were above the clouds now. It wasn't like he could escape and abandon me in this sleek, shiny airplane. Could he?

A fine layer of sweat slicked the underside of my thighs and collected under my armpits. The sweat of fear.

The seat beside me shifted and I turned, relieved that Oliver hadn't parachuted out the emergency exit or something.

Only it wasn't Oliver. It was Princess Isabella Victoria of the hot-pink Converse sneakers and mega-huge castle. But instead of her defiant gaze, she had a kind smile.

"Hello," she said. "I don't think we've had the pleasure of an introduction."

"Uh . . . "

She laughed and shook her head. "Sorry. It always takes me a bit to shift out of royalty speak. What I meant to say is, like, hey."

"Hey," I said.

"What's your name?"

"Abby. I mean, Abigail Jane Herman, Your, um, Royal Highness?"

"Please. Call me Bells. Just not Belle. It's bad enough being a princess; I don't need people thinking I'm trying to be all, like, 'Save the beast! Save the beast!'"

I laughed, forgetting for a moment about my sweaty thighs and armpits. Princess Isabella—I mean, Bells—was waving her hands in front of her face like she was trying to scare away an imaginary beast.

"I always hated that scene in the movie where Belle had to kiss the beast," I said.

"Totally," said Bells. "I mean, kissing my dog? Completely okay. But beast kissing? Not okay under any circumstances!"

"So true!"

By the time Oliver came back, Bells and I were so deep in discussion about all the terrible creatures who princesses have to kiss in movies and books that I forgot I'd ever been desperate for him to stay. We kept talking until Oliver tapped Bells on the shoulder to reclaim his seat.

"See you when we land, Abby," said Bells as she waved good-bye.

As Oliver fastened his seat belt, I replayed my conversation with a real live princess. It had gone well. Great, even. It was only one conversation with one famous kid, but it was a start. Maybe this was going to be okay.

"Oliver," I said. "What do you think happens when we land?"

"Well, first we walk across the landing strip to camp. Then we unpack our belongings in our assigned cabins. Then the lunch bell rings and—"

"Wait a second," I interrupted. "Have you been to Camp Famous before?"

"Well, yes," said Oliver.

"How? We didn't have Ms. McIntyre last year. Why would she get you a place?"

"There's something you need to know, Abby." Oliver paused. He fiddled with a button on his shirt. He rubbed his palms against his pants. Finally he said, "I am known by another name."

Kids at school had a lot of unkind names for Oliver Frank: *nerd, loser, dweeb*. I'd even heard him called *dorksicle* once or twice. But something told me Oliver wasn't talking about those sorts of names.

"Have you heard of Francis Oliver," he continued, "the world-famous reporter?"

"No, what does he have to do with . . . wait a second. Francis Oliver. Oliver Frank. Are you two people in one?"

I leaned my head back. I wanted the hard thud of a wall. Something that stood a chance of waking me up from what had to be a super-weird dream. Did Oliver Frank actually belong at Camp Famous?

Instead, my head sank into the cushioned leather headrest.

"I'm only one person," said Oliver. "But my work appears under the name Francis Oliver. Are you sure it doesn't sound familiar?"

"Never heard of him. I mean, you. I mean, whatever."

"So you don't read the *New York Times*?"

"Nope."

"The *Philadelphia Inquirer*?"

"Never."

"The *Boston Globe*?"

"Oliver! I'm eleven. Do you think I read those things?"

"Well, if you did read them, then you would know that I, Francis Oliver, report on the youth experience in today's technologically saturated and highly pressured, achievement-oriented environment."

"Come again?"

"I write about what it's like to be a kid today."

"Ah, gotcha." I paused, letting this sink in.

Oliver removed his glasses and wiped the lenses with the edge of his shirt.

"Oliver," I said. "Did it ever occur to you that you might not be the best person to write about how it feels to be a regular kid?"

"Yes, Abby. Every single day."

A voice came over the plane's speaker. We were touching down in just a few minutes. Which left only a little bit of time to process a big piece of information, and make an even bigger decision.

Oliver Frank was famous for being a writer named Francis Oliver. Ms. McIntyre hadn't asked her brother to let Oliver into Camp Famous so he could meet a new group of kids. He'd gotten in the regular way, by deserving it.

Which meant I was the only non-famous kid on the entire plane. Once everyone found out, I would be the girl on the outside hoping to be let in, just like at school. It would be recess all day long.

How was I going to finally make friends, maybe even a best friend, if I started off differently than everyone else?

Mom's words mixed with the rumble of the airplane wheels dropping. *Abby, if those kids have any brains inside their famous heads, they are going to love you. Just be yourself. You are perfect exactly as you are.*

I wanted to believe Mom. She was smart. She was strong. But when it came to understanding my friendship problems, she was almost too smart. Too strong. Mom acted like there was an easy answer. Some way to plan a path out of my loneliness, which never worked.

The airplane tilted. A slice of land came into view.

"Oliver," I said. "I need your help. I need to be famous."

"No, you don't, Abby. It might sound weird, but no one really cares about being famous at camp. It's supposed to be a break from all that."

"That's because they *are* famous, Oliver. They're already part of the group. Even you're part of the group. If the other kids find out that I'm regular, they'll treat me like it."

"You're not regular, Abby," said Oliver. "You're awesome."

"Yeah, right."

"Abby—"

I shook my head. Oliver and I had been in the same school since kindergarten. We weren't always in the same class, but he knew me. Oliver may have had two lives, but I only had one. This was my chance.

"Oliver, please. Help me think."

"Okay, fine," said Oliver. "You're really good in language arts. And you're always reading books. Tell them you're a famous writer. Like me. Except you write made-up stories, not newspaper articles."

"No," I said. "They might want to see something I've written. There's no way—"

I thought about my notebook tucked inside the backpack at my feet. All the thoughts and observations that no famous kid would ever write down. Recess embarrassment. Being left out of candy-filled sleepovers. Fear of never-ending friendship failure.

"One minute to landing," announced the pilot.

I had to think fast. "Why can't I write newspaper articles, like you?"

Oliver shook his head. "Famous kids don't like reporters. They trust me because they know I only write about the youth experience in today's technologically saturated—"

"I remember," I interrupted.

The wheels of the plane dropped to the ground. The famous kids behind us began to clap. The sound of me running out of time.

"Okay," I said. "Fine. I'll tell them I write books, but under a different name that I don't want to reveal."

"I don't know, Abby. It's not that easy to be two people at once. It's a lot to keep track of. I've had years of practice."

"Oliver, Kai Carter is famous partly for chewing on the strings of his sweatshirt. Princess Isabella is famous partly for wearing hot-pink sneakers under her ball gowns. You're apparently famous for writing articles that no one reads."

"Well, that's not quite—"

"Please, Oliver. Just let me try. I really need this to work."

"Okay, Abby. Your secret is safe with me."

The plane rolled to a smooth stop. The front doors opened right away. Warm summer air flowed down the aisle as everyone stood and gathered their bags. Everyone except Oliver, that is.

"Come on, Oliver," I said. "We have to get off."

Oliver tucked one hand into his lap and closed his eyes. "I pinched my finger on the seat belt buckle," he said. "Go without me. I need a minute to recover."

It was just a finger. It's not like he was bleeding. And I really wanted to see what was outside. So with one last glance at Oliver, I lifted my backpack to my shoulders and walked off the plane. As I stepped from the staircase to the ground, Bells came up beside me.

"I'm so excited," she said. "No pictures. No posing. No waiting and waiting and even more waiting for an entire three weeks!"

"Waiting for what?" I asked.

"Everything," said Bells, throwing her head back and opening her arms wide. "Carriage processions, knighting ceremonies, dress fittings, tea with old people who sip super slow and refold their napkins for fun."

Bells bent in half like an inflatable doll that had lost its air. Then she shot back up. "By the way, I forgot to ask what you're famous for."

Ha! Oliver had said that no one at Camp Famous cared about fame. But I knew it mattered.

Even though I had a plan, saying the words out loud was terrifying. There would be no going back. I stalled. "Who, me?"

There was no one else nearby so the question sounded as awkward as I felt. But Bells just nodded, as if being famous was no big deal. As if, *duh*, of course there was something special about me.

I glanced over my right shoulder. No Oliver. I glanced over my left shoulder. No Oliver. Even though he'd promised to keep my secret, I was still worried about his reaction to hearing me lie out loud. Oliver Frank was not very good at subtle facial reactions.

"It's okay," said Bells softly. "You won't hurt my feelings or anything. I get that I don't really belong at Camp Famous. Not the way the rest of you do."

Princess Isabella Victoria of magazine covers and ball gowns as poufy as clouds thought *she* didn't belong at Camp Famous?

My feet slowed, as if my sneakers had just been filled with the gold bricks that were totally hidden deep inside Bells's palace somewhere. Bells looked so withdrawn that I was tempted to tell her the truth. Nothing would make Bells realize how completely she belonged like knowing how much I did not. But I stuck to my plan. I spit out my lie. "I'm a writer. Of books that a lot of kids read."

Bells tilted her head, considering. She smiled. "Oh, cool."

"Yeah," I said. "Cool."

Bells and I walked across the landing strip as if nothing majorly major had just happened. She didn't ask the titles of any of my nonexistent books. Or the plots of the stories that I had never written.

My lie drifted into the cloudless summer sky.

Maybe the real explanation was that no one at Camp Famous cared what you were famous for as long as you were famous for something. Which meant I'd made the right decision.

Around a bend the entrance came into view. I'd spent weeks imagining Camp Summerah. In my mind it looked just like Camp Longatocket. The lake. The cabins. The signs.

Camp Famous was kinda, sorta, mostly like that. There was a wide field with cabins dotted along the edge and tall evergreen trees beyond. There was a lake with wooden docks in a U shape.

But it was like comparing the tech classroom in the new wing of school to the art classroom in the old wing of school. Everything at Camp Famous was cleaner, sharper, with a bit of a glow.

The signs were printed in a crisp font instead of painted by hand. Out past the U-shaped docks was a second floating dock with a huge metal slide. I imagined screaming in joyful fear as my body flew down the slide and landed in the lake with a giant splash.

We continued walking until we reached the center of the field, where a man stood with his thumbs tucked into his shoulder straps. He looked so much like Ms. McIntyre that I had to resist the urge to wave.

"Welcome, welcome, welcome," he said, the words piling on top of one another. "It's so, so, so awesome to see all you campers."

"That's Joe," whispered Bells. "He runs Camp Famous."

Joe. Joe McIntyre, who knew my real story.

Did Joe spend a lot of time with the campers? Or was he more like a school principal who worked mostly in an office? Maybe Oliver would know.

I looked around but got distracted trying to figure out where I'd seen a boy with paint splattered across his shorts (TV? The movies? A movie that I'd watched on TV?). Then Bells tapped me on the shoulder, drawing me back to the present.

"Joe always speaks in groups of three," she whispered. "Listen."

"We've got some new stuff, we've got some old stuff, and we've got some in-between stuff. But the most important part of camp remains the same—fun, fun, fun."

I'm pretty sure that Joe went on to describe the specific type of fun waiting for us. But I was so busy trying not to giggle as Bells counted to three with her fingers that I didn't hear the details.

It had been a long time since I'd fought that hard not to laugh. The effort made my stomach clench in the best possible way.

"Your parents would totally flip out if they were here right now," said Bells. "Joe was a TV star a super-long time ago and all the old people know him."

My parents. I looked to the sky. Were they still in the air? Or had their flight landed, too?

And what about Grandma? Last night when I'd called her to say good-bye, she'd reminded me over and over that the camp director had her phone number in case of emergency. Maybe I should also write it down someplace safe, just in case? Grandma never seemed worried about me, even when she knew I was having a hard time at school. She must have known that I was headed somewhere other than normal sleepover camp. With normal kids.

A lot of people had told a lot of lies to get me to this point: Ms. McIntyre, my parents, Grandma.

There must have been secret phone calls and emails and plans. The electric energy of it buzzing around my house. Visible to everyone except me.

The familiar heavy feeling of being left out seeped into my body. But instead of weighing me down, the way it sometimes did at school, I stood taller.

None of those people were here to tell me what to do. I was in charge of what happened next.

When Joe called my name for cabin assignments, pointing me toward a counselor wearing a wooden medallion around her neck that read "Carly," I threaded my hands through the straps of my backpack, my notebook tucked safely inside, and jogged over.

It was time to try out the new Abby.

There were four cabin groups. Two for boys. Two for girls.

Joe continued to call out names, and the main group grew smaller. Gathered with me around Carly were three other girls: a girl twisting her long wavy hair around her finger named Hazel Fair; a girl with a perfect ballerina bun named Willa Jones; and a girl wearing black boots with pink neon laces named Shira Gumm.

Bells was still in the main group, waiting for her cabin assignment. Then Joe said, "Princess

Isabella Victoria, you can head on over to Carly,"
and Bells came running over to our group.

Hazel, Willa, Shira and I had been standing
still, evenly spaced like chess pieces on our own
squares. Once Bells arrived, it felt like the game
could begin. Bells hugged Shira and Hazel in a
giddy way that made it clear they had all been to
Camp Famous before. She smiled at Willa and told
her to please call her Bells. Then she bumped her
shoulder against mine and squealed.

"Hooray! We're in the same cabin!"

"All right, girls," said Carly once Bells finished
all her greetings. "That's all of us. Follow me to
Cabin Tranquility."

Bells walked in between Shira and Hazel. Willa
and I followed behind. The three of them were
shoulder to shoulder, deep in conversation.

"Is this your first time here?" asked Willa.

I nodded.

"Same," said Willa. "Do you think it's going to
be fun?"

"Definitely." I paused. "Do you?"

"Probably," said Willa. "At least, that's what everyone promised. But you know how they are. Especially when it comes to the whole you-only-get-to-be-a-kid-once thing."

Willa could have been referring to her parents, but her mocking tone made it seem like she was speaking about a group of bossy grown-ups.

I'd never considered being talked into going to sleepover camp instead of begging to go. But as we continued along a path that was covered in wood chips, Willa wrapped her arms around her body as if she was trying to keep our new surroundings out. Or, maybe, keep her feelings tucked in.

"You didn't want to come?" I asked.

"It's not that I didn't want to try camp. It sounds fun and all. But I didn't want to leave my dance studio at home. I'm playing the role of Clara in the new *Nutcracker* movie, and filming starts in September. If I don't dance every day, it's going to show on screen. No one understands how important my training is."

"Oh," I said, hoping it sounded like I understood when I really meant it like: Oh, wow!

"They promised there'd be lots of places to dance here," continued Willa. "But I don't see any. Do you?"

Willa's chin, which had been raised to keep her perfect posture, began to tremble. I scanned the buildings within view. Across the field was a large structure that looked big enough for the entire camp to gather inside—like maybe a dining hall. On either side of it were several buildings the size of large sheds. I doubted any of them were dance studios.

"I'm not sure," I said.

"I knew they were lying just to get me to say yes. I don't know what I'm going to do."

Willa was wearing sneakers and jean shorts, but her body looked ready to leap into the air at any second. Even though I was certain that she must be an amazing dancer, I sensed that wasn't what she wanted to hear. While I had no idea how it felt to dread sleepover camp, I knew how it felt to be lied to. Just a few hours ago I'd thought that I was going to Camp Summerah.

"I'm really sorry," I said.

And even though it wasn't a solution, Willa must have heard how deeply I meant the words. She relaxed her arms and smiled. "Thanks."

"I'm terrible at dance, but if you want me to help you practice your lines, I'm really good at reading."

"Really? Cool. I brought my script. Do you mind playing all the parts? Even the mean ones?"

I squinted my eyes, joined my fingers in a steeple grip, and dropped my voice. "I love mean characters."

Willa laughed. "We might need to work on your accent. But I'll take all the help I can get."

We continued talking until Carly stopped in front of the first cabin in a row of four. "Welcome to

Cabin Tranquility, girls," she said. "Your home for the next three weeks."

My jaw dropped. Cabin Tranquility was the cabin of my sleepover camp dreams. There were two wide steps leading to a covered front porch. A screen door painted in dark green trim. A wood-shingled roof.

I didn't notice that I was standing in frozen awe until Bells pulled my arm as she began to skip up the steps.

"Come on, Abby! Let's find our beds."

I walked up the steps and through the screen door. The walls, the ceiling, the floor—they were all made of different types of wood. Sunlight and warm summer air drifted in from the open windows. The main room was square with a circular woven rug in the center. Toward the back was a bathroom area with two sinks, one shower, and one toilet stall.

It smelled like wet leaves and sunblock.

There were five empty beds spaced along the

walls, each with a stack of wooden shelves. At the end of each bed were duffel bags or, in Bells's case, a collection of brown leather trunks with her initials printed in gold. My navy duffel was next to her trunk collection.

"Yay," said Bells. "We get to sleep next to each other."

I smiled. It was as if the sunlight from the window was shining only on me.

I unpacked carefully, making sure my clothes were arranged in neat piles, my socks and underwear stowed in the plastic bin Mom and I had selected at Target. Once my duffel bag was empty I slid it under my bed. I wasn't sure what to do with my backpack, which had my notebook, Wilbur, and some books inside.

Should I take my notebook out and place it on the shelf closest to my pillow?

Maybe. But the cabin was small. The beds close together. I immediately understood why Mom had been so intent on labeling all my clothes and belongings. It was only a matter of time before all our things got jumbled up.

I imagined the hot-pink sequins on the notebook's cover catching the light and shooting sparkles across the wooden room. Someone might follow the light trail back to my notebook and ask to see it.

I wanted to keep my notebook private just as much as I wanted to write in it. So I left my notebook in my backpack and tucked the backpack under my bed.

It only took a few minutes to realize that was the right decision. Shira threw a towel to Hazel, saying that she'd accidentally taken it home last summer. Hazel threw it back, saying that it smelled like it had been sitting in Shira's bag *since* last summer. Bells twirled around, placing sprigs of dried lavender tied with green satin ribbons on everyone's pillows like a fairy dropping magical gifts. Gifts from the royal housekeeper, Bells explained.

There were bathing-suit bottoms hanging from

bedposts and hairbrushes overturned on the floor like sleeping porcupines. Willa rolled out a yoga mat beside her bed, and Shira flopped down on it pretending to take a nap. Willa pretended not to notice and stretched into a downward dog over Shira's body.

It was chaotic and cozy.

I would have been happy to stay there forever if Carly hadn't tapped me on the shoulder and reminded me that there was even more camp right outside the cabin door.

"**W**hy doesn't Hazel give you a quick tour before lunch since you're both unpacked," said Carly.

Carly's voice was cheery, but her forehead was dotted with sweat from trying to maintain some teensy bit of order as everyone unpacked their belongings. She clearly thought fewer girls in the cabin would help. I followed Hazel outside into the sunshine.

We walked in silence past three cabins that looked just like Cabin Tranquility with name signs that read "Destiny," "Serenity," and "Harmony."

Beyond the cabins were a collection of wooden buildings called the Art Hut, the Music Studio, and the Zendom.

Hazel explained that they were where a lot of the daytime activities took place.

"What's the Zendom?" I asked.

"Where Joe offers meditation classes. They're optional, and no one really goes. You're not allowed to wear shoes in there, and Joe's feet are . . ." Hazel pinched her nose and swatted the air.

The movement blew some of the hair away from her face. As I suspected, Hazel was just as pretty as she was quiet. Not a boring quiet, though. The kind of quiet that made me want to lean in and listen. We continued on to the basketball court, the tennis courts, and a sandy circle that had a metal pole with a ball attached to a long string.

"Tetherball," said Hazel. "Everyone was obsessed last year."

I nodded. If everyone was obsessed, then I should definitely pretend to know what it was.

"I'll show you my favorite place in all of camp," said Hazel.

We headed toward a bench that faced the lake. I paused to take in the metal slide at the far end of the swim area. The wooden dock at its base bobbed gently in the water. Hazel must not have noticed me stop. She continued walking to the bench.

"Oh my gosh," she said, bringing her hand to her chest as I sat down next to her. "You scared me."

"Sorry?"

Had she forgotten about me? It had only been a few seconds.

"It's okay," said Hazel. "I just don't like it when people come up behind me."

That was understandable. I wasn't sure what Hazel was famous for, but people probably ran up to her on the street and asked to take her picture all the time. Maybe she was an actor on one of the many TV shows that Quinn loved but Mom and Dad refused to let me watch?

I didn't want to come right out and ask. So instead I said, "One time someone came up behind me while I was drinking milk at a restaurant. I was so startled that I snorted white bubbles out my nose."

"Yikes," said Hazel. "Did anyone catch it on camera?"

Hazel's eyes were wide and concerned, as if maybe the video had gone viral and I was known all over the world as Snort Girl.

"Um, I don't think so."

Hazel exhaled. "Phew. That's the last thing you want. I'm sure you've seen my turkey video?"

I shook my head, clueless as to what Hazel was talking about.

"My mom took the video when I was four years old," said Hazel. "We'd learned this song about a turkey from Albuquerque in preschool and I was singing it for my family at the Thanksgiving table. Just as I finished, my dad walked out carrying a turkey on a platter, all roasted and shiny. I made the happy song/dead turkey connection and broke into tears."

"Makes sense," I said. "Dead turkeys are . . . dead turkeys. They're super sad."

Hazel smiled. "Exactly. But my mom got the whole thing on video and posted it on her blog. Next thing I knew, I was flying to New York City to be interviewed on all these talk shows."

"Wow."

"I know, right? The worst."

I'd actually been thinking that being interviewed on TV sounded super cool. But I pressed my lips together and nodded.

"So you're famous because of the turkey video?" I asked.

"I guess," said Hazel. "I mean, that's how it started. After that video my mom's blog got more and more popular. Then she expanded to all the different social media channels. At first I didn't even realize that my mom was posting pictures of me to her bazillions of followers online. I thought she just liked photography and fancy cameras. But now sharing my life is her job. The one that pays her money that we need to live. And I'm stuck."

Hazel sighed. Even in her gloom she was so darn pretty. Her eyes dreamy. Her frown delicate. "But at least I get to come here," she continued. "It always takes me a few days to remember that my mom's not around to take my picture when I'm not looking. That for three weeks I'm totally free."

Hazel wasn't jumpy at the thought of adoring fans. She was jumpy at the thought of her own mom. "She really posts your picture without your permission?" I asked. "That's so bad."

"All day long. At home no one understands. Some kids treat me like I'm all snobby because I always have new trendy clothes or whatever. But here everyone gets it. They know that my mom doesn't actually buy the clothes. Companies send them to her so she can take my picture and share it." Hazel exhaled. "Thanks for listening."

I nodded. I didn't *totally* understand. But sitting

next to Hazel, watching her twist the strings of her cutoff jean shorts into tight coils as she spoke, I could sense how trapped she felt.

"I get it," I said, smiling. "Just like everyone else."

A bell clanged from across the field.

"Time for lunch," said Hazel. "Come on."

The dining hall was the large building that I'd noticed earlier at the far end of the field. Hazel and I walked through the double doors together.

Not only did the dining hall look different from the school cafeteria, with wooden tables and long benches instead of plastic chairs. It *felt* different. No one was saving seats. The dining hall seemed like a nice sunny place to eat. Not a place to survive.

"Abby!" called Oliver from across the room. "Over here!"

I waved, hoping that would be enough. But

Oliver began making large circular motions with his arms, signaling for me to come over.

"I'll be right back," I told Hazel.

If I was going to pull off this belonging thing, Oliver was going to have to tone it down. No one could know that we knew each other from home.

"Hey, Abby," said Oliver. "Are you okay? Do you like your cabin? Is your bed comfortable? Do you want me to show you around this afternoon during free time? There's a reading spot near the campfire circle that feels like an earth hammock. You'll love it. We could each bring a book and—"

"That's okay," I interrupted. "Hazel just gave me a tour."

"Did she show you the earth hammock?" Oliver scrunched his eyebrows together, doubtful. His glasses slipped down his nose.

"How's your finger?" I asked, trying to change the subject.

"My finger? What finger?" Oliver wiggled his fingers in front of his eyes. They all seemed perfectly fine.

"The one you hurt on the plane."

"Oh, that finger. I think it's all better now. Thank you for asking, Abby. But back to the earth hammock. I'm fairly certain that no one else knows about it. I discovered it all by myself on the second-to-last—"

"Oliver, I'm fine."

The words came out sharper than I intended. Oliver was making me nervous. He seemed like the same exact Oliver from school. The same jiggly energy. The same speedy brain power mixed with a tinge of cluelessness.

If Oliver was exactly the same person, maybe I was, too. I needed space to figure out how to be famous Abby. Oliver Frank was not good at space.

"Listen, Oliver," I whispered. "Can we pretend that we don't know each other?"

"Like, ignore each other? As if the other person doesn't exist?"

"No, I mean, we can talk to each other. But let's start as if we're two strangers who met on the plane. Just like everyone else."

"But I'm already friends with a lot of people here." Oliver began pointing at kids around the dining hall, listing their names, ending with Kai Carter, who just happened to be walking past.

"Did someone say my name?" asked Kai, sliding to a stop in his black-and-white checkered sneakers. His hair fell across his forehead in a smooth swoop.

"I was just talking to a new camper," said Oliver. "Her name is Abby. At least, I think that's her name."

It was impossible to ignore the sarcasm in Oliver's voice. The way he stretched out the syllables in my name and rounded them off with a hint of hurt. I was used to Oliver shrugging things off. I'd certainly seen him do it at school. Had I really hurt his feelings?

I promised myself that I'd make it up to him. Once things settled down. Once everyone got to know the famous me. Once . . .

"Do you guys want to sit together?" asked Kai.

. . . once I had lunch with Kai Carter! After that I would totally figure out how to make things right with Oliver.

It had been a long time since breakfast, and the food at Camp Famous was amazing. I pushed my tray through the buffet line of nachos dripping with cheese, chicken fingers with three kinds of dipping sauce, and French fries so crispy that they crunched between my teeth before coating my mouth in soft potato perfection. For dessert there were mini cupcakes with a single gummy bear sitting atop the icing peak.

Kai, Oliver, and I sat at one end of a rectangular table. Bells, Willa, and Hazel sat at the other. Bells made kissing faces at me when Kai wasn't looking. You would think a princess would have better table manners!

"So, uh, Kai," I said. "What's your favorite song?"

I was trying to make a subtle stop-embarrassing-me face at Bells when Kai surprised me by answering, "Tough one. I'm going to have to go with 'The Itsy-bitsy Spider.'"

I almost choked on my gummy bear. "As in, the spider who climbed up the water spout?"

"'Then down came the rain and washed the spider out,'" sang Kai.

Not only could Kai make a grungy red sweatshirt look like the hottest fashion item, he could make a nursery rhyme sound like a top hit. I'd never felt such sympathy for that determined little spider.

"I know it's a little kid song," continued Kai, "but my grandma used to sing it to me when she came to visit. It just makes me happy."

"That's how I feel about 'How Much Is That Doggie in the Window?'"

"The one with the waggly tail?" asked Kai, smiling.

"Yes! Because he sounds so cute and lovable and what if he's not for sale? That would be so sad."

"Tragic," agreed Kai.

"My grandma used to sing that song to me before bed," I said. "One time she recorded it so my mom could play it for me when I missed her."

"Same!" said Kai.

"Your mom played recordings of *my* grandma?"

It was a risky joke. What if Kai Carter thought I was serious? What if he pulled up the hood of his red sweatshirt, tightened the drawstrings, and never spoke to me again?

But then, after the longest pause of my entire life, Kai laughed. "That would be major-league creepy."

And I almost died with relief.

When lunch ended, we carried our plates and silverware to the back of the dining hall, sorting them into large containers of soapy water. Joe stood at the doors to the dining hall, directing everyone back to their cabins for rest hour.

There was moaning and groaning, as if Joe had announced a surprise math quiz. But I couldn't wait to get back to Cabin Tranquility. Rest hour was probably my best chance to write in my notebook.

My fingers twitched just thinking about all that I needed to get down.

Dear Notebook,

It's finally quiet in here. It took a little while to get settled because Bells was making funny faces and Shira was throwing tiny balls of paper at Bells to make her stop. Then Willa did a stretch where she pulled her leg over her head. Bells tried to copy Willa and crashed to the floor.

Rest hour is the one time of the day when we're supposed to be quiet and stay on our own beds. So Carly got annoyed (but in a funny pretend way), which made us laugh even harder!

Now everyone is lying down. Sorry if my handwriting is messy. It's hard to write on a bed and I feel a little shaky. The quiet is making me realize how much has happened since this morning.

Like, there's an actual princess right next to me. I'm not starting with Bells just because her bed is the closest.

She's the kind of person you start with, no matter what. She's butterfly-ish, like Marin. Always fluttering around from person to person.

The ball gown she wore on that magazine cover must have been super uncomfortable because she's not as intimidating as she looked. Like right now she's tracing the words of her graphic novel with one finger and flipping each page with the tip of another finger. It's taking her forever to turn the pages.

How is it possible that Bells thinks she doesn't belong at Camp Famous? She's a princess who was on the cover of a magazine! Next to her bed is a picture of her family on top of a snow-covered mountain. They're not wearing crowns or tiaras, just regular ski clothes. But you can tell that they're powerful just by looking at them. Her older brother is holding his skis in his hands like they weigh nothing at all.

Across from me is Willa. She's rolling out her feet and

ankles. Probably for ballet. Willa got tricked into coming to camp. Kind of like me, I guess. But that might be the only thing we have in common. I can't imagine loving something so much that you'd rather be doing it than be at sleepover camp. But when you watch Willa, it makes sense. She's graceful even when she walks.

Hazel is in the bed next to Willa. I think she's writing a letter. She keeps tearing her paper in half and reaching for a new sheet. Hazel is really nice even if she sometimes spaces out a little. Or maybe she more sinks in a little. Like right now she's curled around whatever she's writing with her blanket over her even though it's summer.

It's weird to feel bad for Hazel because she has the coolest clothes. But she's also really jumpy. Not like Willa, who could leap into the air with her legs in a split, but a scared kind of jumpy. I can't imagine bazillions of strangers seeing pictures of me. Although maybe that's just part of being famous. Maybe the scary part is that Hazel's mom is the one taking all the pictures.

The last girl is Shira. She's on my side of the cabin next to Bells, so I can't see her very well. I don't know what she's famous for, but I think it's something smart. Probably involving math. I'll let you know more about her as soon as I figure it out.

Our counselor, Carly, is getting up from her bed so I have to go now. Sorry to put you back in my backpack under the bed. It's the safest place for you. I promise to write in you every day and give you all the camp news!

Love,

Abby

At the end of rest hour, Carly asked us to gather on the front porch for a cabin meeting. She explained that starting tomorrow there would be a regular camp schedule of breakfast, cabin cleanup, morning activity, free time, lunch, rest hour, afternoon activity, free time, dinner, and evening activity.

At every change a counselor would ring the large bell by the dining hall. We would choose our morning activities at morning circle and our afternoon activities at afternoon circle. Most times we could pick whatever activity we wanted, but sometimes we would be doing things together as a cabin.

Carly tapped out the daily events on her fingers—a nice orderly list of campy fun. When she finished, Carly clapped her hands together and said, "But right now we need to report to the lake for a swim test. Who's ready to cool off? It's hot out today!"

I was so ready to cool off. The nervous sweat from the airplane had dried on my skin. My shorts were practically sticking to my thighs. I loved to swim in the pool at Grandma's retirement village. I imagined that a lake would be even better. No chlorine taste. No lanes roped off with plastic dividers. Hopefully no fish.

Plus that huge slide into the water!

We changed into our bathing suits and grabbed our towels. All five of us walked down the path that led to the lake. The other cabins arrived at the same time. I waved at Oliver and he waved back, which I took as a good sign.

I still owed Oliver an apology from what I'd said

at lunch. Maybe he'd already forgotten about it?

I placed my towel on one of the benches that lined the sand. Bells raised her hand to block the sun from her eyes and looked around the beachfront.

"I don't see any inflatable swans," she said. "Do you? There were three last summer, but they didn't last very long."

"What happened to them?"

"This boy named Archer got to them. He'd won some television talent show contest for juggling swords while blowing fireballs, and he had major anger issues. He came down to the lake early one morning and began hurling stolen kitchen knives at those poor plastic swans. They didn't stand a chance. He decapitated each one on the very first try."

"He chopped off their heads?"

Bells nodded and drew her hand swiftly in front of her neck. "Joe called for the evacuation helicopter straight away. Archer was off the premises before the swans even sank."

Yikes, I thought. Poor swans. Then I asked, "What's the evacuation helicopter?"

"The standby helicopter that transports people off the camp grounds. If anyone sneaks into camp or presents a threat, the helicopter swoops in and sweeps them away into the clouds. Just a standard safety precaution. You know how it is. One can never be too careful."

I nodded, even though I had no idea how it is. We had an alarm at my house, but we hadn't used it since the time that Dad, seeing a hummingbird flitting away in the backyard, ran into the glass door in excitement. The shattered glass was replaced with a flimsy screen. The alarm sensor was never fixed.

Why bother?

But I thought about the wall of photographers at the airport. The shouts that echoed down the corridor. The big dudes with earpieces on the airplane.

As Joe stepped onto the dock and motioned

for everyone to quiet down, I looked into the sky, imagining a helicopter swooping down and landing on the beach. A helicopter might seem normal to Bells, but it wasn't normal for me. I pictured the whirling blades. The strong wind gusts that I'd seen in movies kicking up the sand.

Even though the sun was glaring, I shivered with fear.

"All righty, all righty, all righty," said Joe. "Water safety is rule number one here at Camp Famous. As returning campers know, in order to be allowed in the lake for free swim, you must complete two full laps across the swim zone. To be permitted to go past the main swim docks for any reason, you must complete four laps. I want to see clear, confident, freestyle strokes. Understood?"

"Are you nervous for the swim test?" whispered Shira as Joe continued to talk about the test.

I was rubbing my arms, trying to smooth the goose bumps that had appeared. Being nervous for a swim test was probably easier for her to understand than being awed by the idea of a helicopter. So I nodded.

And I actually was a little nervous. When Carly said we were taking a swim test, I didn't realize that all the other cabins would be taking it at the same time. That was a lot of famous eyes watching me swim. And because I only swam for fun, I'd never learned any formal strokes.

I'd seen Olympic swimmers do the freestyle stroke on TV, of course. But I'd never tried it myself.

"I'm nervous, too," said Shira. "I didn't get to go on the slide last year. Not one single time. But I grew an inch and a half since last summer, so hopefully I'm strong enough now to pass. Do you want to go last together?"

As Joe walked to the far end of the dock, Shira and I took small steps back from the rest of the kids. Joe had a whistle around his neck and a clipboard in his hand.

Hazel, Willa, and a boy named Cameron Craze (who was responsible for a viral dance that involved a whirlwind series of hand claps and hip thrusts) volunteered to go first. They wrapped their toes around the wooden edge of the dock and stacked their hands over their heads.

Joe called out: "Three, two, one, go!"

They each completed their first two laps with ease, then confirmed that they wanted to try for four. All three were barely out of breath when they climbed back onto the dock and accepted Joe's high five of congratulations.

And on it went. Not everyone was as graceful as Willa, or as fast as Cameron Craze. Bells rested for a bit between laps, and Kai swam on such a sharp diagonal that he had to backtrack almost an extra lap worth of strokes.

But they all managed to complete four freestyle laps to Joe's satisfaction.

The last ones left were me, Shira, and Oliver. We walked onto the dock as everyone else waited on the sand, wrapped in their towels like happy, accomplished burritos.

My heart thumped as I curled my toes around the edge of the dock.

Joe began his countdown. "Three, two, one, go!"

I jumped into the water and started to swim. The first lap was okay. I imitated what the other kids had done. I lifted my arms, elbows first. I flutter kicked my legs. I breathed on one side then the next.

But by the time I started my second lap, I was just so tired.

It was both impossible to continue and impossible to stop.

I lifted my head to check on Shira and Oliver. Oliver was in front of me. His strokes were robotic but effective. If a rope had magically appeared, I totally would have tied myself to Oliver and begged him to drag me forward.

Shira, somehow, was behind me. She was tossing her body in all sorts of ways that resulted in very little forward movement. But we both managed to complete lap two, returning to where

Joe was crouching on the dock, waving his arms for us to continue.

Oliver had already begun lap three.

"You've got this!" said Joe. "Just two more laps and you're cleared for the deep water! Go! Go! Go!"

My heart was on fire. My arms were on fire. My legs were on fire.

That was a whole lot of heat for a chilly lake.

I lifted my arms onto the dock. It was either take a break or die.

I dropped my forehead to my arms in defeat. In exhaustion. In embarrassment.

Shira hoisted her body next to mine on the dock, her shoulders rising and falling as she struggled for air. "Can't. Go. Any. Farther."

"Same."

"Okay," said Joe. "Good job, girls. Catch your breath, and you can always try again later. Anytime you want."

I glanced at the beach where Bells was dragging her fingers through the sand. Hazel was talking to Kai. Willa and Cameron were doing some fast hand-slapping dance moves.

The day had been full of so many new experiences. But what passed over me as the top half of my body lay draped across the warm wooden dock, my legs dangling in the water, was so familiar it was almost comforting.

It was the sticky, lonely, left-behind feeling of not being good enough.

This time, at least, I wasn't all alone. I turned my cheek to face Shira and rested it on the dock.

"We're the only ones who can't use the slide," I said.

Shira gave a small nod as the weight of disappointment settled over both of us. Then she said, "If it makes you feel better, statistically speaking, the probability of every person passing a test of any kind is unlikely. If it's a true test, then the presiding assumption is that some attempts will be unsuccessful. Otherwise, the test is a waste of resources that could and should be redirected to worthier endeavors."

"That doesn't really make me feel better."

She sighed. "Me neither."

After our breathing slowed, Shira dipped her finger into the water and began to draw a symbol on a dry area of the dock. It appeared to be a cross between a number and a letter. Definitely something math-y.

"What is that?" I asked.

"A new chemical equation that I'm thinking about. If I don't write the components down, they get stuck in my head and pile on top of each other like theorem rocks."

I wasn't sure what a chemical equation or a theorem was, but I understood things getting stuck in your head. And how writing them down helped them to shift. Feel a little lighter.

After all, it was one of the things Grandma said to me when she gave me my notebook for my birthday. *Sometimes it helps to put your thoughts down on paper.*

"That's how I feel about writing," I said.

Shira wiped her wet bangs off her forehead. She blinked away a stray drop of water and said, "Are you a famous writer?"

Uh-oh.

No one had asked about my claim to fame since Bells when we got off the plane. Not Hazel on the bench. Or Kai at lunch. No one else in my cabin.

I stumbled getting the lie out. "Well . . . it's kind of like . . . it's a little complicated because—"

"It's okay," interrupted Shira. "You don't have to tell me if you write under another name or whatever. I'm a U.F.C., too. It's honestly better. Did you see that girl at the airport almost faint when Kai Carter walked by? She came close to hitting her head on a luggage cart. His just being alive causes actual bodily harm."

"Right," I said, pretending I had a clue what a U.F.C was. "Because U.F.C.s don't cause bodily harm. It's kind of our thing?"

"At least not in public, since no one knows our

faces. That's the best part about being famous *and* unrecognizable."

Famous and unrecognizable. Unrecognizable and famous. Maybe that explained the *U* and the *F*. But what about the *C*? I hoped it didn't stand for chemistry. Or crazy smart.

It was time for a teensy dose of honesty.

"Is it weird that no told me I was a U.F.C.?" I asked.

Shira shook her head. "No one told me my first year, either. I only saw it this year when my parents were filling out the camp application. There was a box to check for what kind of camper you were. Recognizable or unrecognizable."

C for "camper"! That made sense.

"What are you famously unrecognizable for?" I asked, trying to roll the conversation like a beach ball back to Shira.

She smiled. "Slime."

"Like *slime* slime?"

The slime craze had hit my school last year. It

began slowly, with gooey white globs inside plastic bags. Then it grew to include beautiful colors stored in labeled containers. And also parties where everyone sank their hands into large bowls of ingredients to mix the perfect combination, squealing with gross delight.

At least, that's what I'd imagined happened at slime parties based on Quinn's braggity bragging. But I never found out for sure.

Slime was the sort of thing that just happened, appearing like an unexpected rain storm on a clear day. But I guess someone had to be the first person to make it. And that someone was lying next to me. The sun warming our backs, failure running through our tired arms and legs.

"I've got something new," said Shira. "It's even cooler."

Competing thoughts entered my brain: *Tell me!* And *Don't ever tell anyone!*

Something cooler than slime would mean more parties that I wasn't invited to.

But Shira continued, "Slime that can burp and fart."

"Fart? Like with a smell? Gross."

"I meant a farting *sound*. Although, adding a release of putrid vapor to my chemical compound is an interesting idea." Shira paused to dip her finger in the lake and draw something on the dock. "My new slime can move, and the movement triggers really gross squishing, squelching noises. It's going to be huge among the younger demographic. Probably a worldwide phenomenon if no other inventor beats me to it. At least, that's what my business manager claims."

"Wow," I said.

Because what else was there to say to the idea of burping slime?

The next morning after breakfast, I was walking across the field back to Cabin Tranquility when I heard someone call, "Abb-y!"

The two syllables rose and fell like a gentle wave. There was only one voice who could make my oh-so-regular name sound like it belonged to someone oh-so-cool.

Kai Carter wanted to talk to me.

I let my cabinmates walk ahead and waited for him to catch up.

"What's up?" I asked.

"I was thinking about you last night."

It helped that Kai was wearing a blue T-shirt. Not his signature red hoodie. His hair was also a little messy. Less swoop, more curls. But even fake-famous me had limits.

Stay calm, I told myself. You are famous. People think about you all the time. This is not a reason to stop breathing.

"Oh, really," I managed to say. "How come?"

"I was trying to fall asleep and 'Twinkle, Twinkle, Little Star' popped into my head. Remember that one?"

"Yes!" I said, relieved. Nursery rhymes I could handle.

"It's no 'Itsy-bitsy Spider,'" said Kai. "But it's still good."

"Or 'Doggie in the Window.' How could you forget about that cute little guy with his waggly tail!"

"Sorry!" said Kai, laughing as he lifted his hands defensively. "My bad!"

I crossed my arms in fake anger. "I'm not sure I'm ready to forgive you."

"Join the club," said Kai, suddenly serious. He kicked the toe of his sneaker into the grass. He was definitely thinking about something heavier than nursery rhymes.

"You know I'm just joking, right? My parents refuse to get a dog. Not even from an animal shelter. They wouldn't care how cute it was or how much it wagged its tail."

"I know," said Kai. "It's not that. You just reminded me of all these people from real life who are mad at me."

I thought about Kai's life. Singing in front of thousands of adoring fans. Being led through cheering crowds by bodyguards. Posing for pictures that were later printed on posters and shirts. I couldn't imagine anyone being *angry* at him.

My confusion must have been obvious, because Kai continued explaining. "Before I left for camp, I told my management team that I want to try writing the songs for my upcoming tour instead of singing lyrics that other people write for me. But my team thinks it's too risky. They don't think I can write anything good enough."

The lyrics to Kai's song about heart-shaped rocks sinking to the bottom of the ocean played in my head. It was Quinn's favorite song. She thought it was so romantic and would bring her hand to her chest every time she sang the line about crying on a surfboard as the sun set over the horizon. Now that I knew Kai, it made sense that he hadn't written that song, or any of the others. He didn't seem like someone who would cry on a surfboard. He seemed like someone who would be looking for the next wave.

"I bet you can write amazing songs," I said.

Kai perked up, his eyes meeting mine. "You think so?"

Someone must have told Kai that I was a famous writer. Why else would he look so hopeful and trusting? But I really did think he could write his own songs. I'd noticed Kai in line for breakfast that morning nodding his head to a beat. When he couldn't fall asleep, he thought about nursery rhymes. Music clearly mattered to him.

"I could, um, read your lyrics sometime. Or listen to them. Whatever."

"Seriously? That would be awesome, Abby. Thanks."

"As long as you don't play favorites with any animals," I said, trying to change the subject. What if Kai asked me for advice about songwriting? Or writing in general?

Kai paused, thinking. "So no 'Mary Had a Little Lamb'? Even though the itsy-bitsy spider would so be friends with that troublemaking lamb."

"I *said*, no playing favorites!"

As Kai and I walked back to our cabins, we tried to figure out how a determined little spider and a pesky lamb could free a dog from a pet store window. Maybe the lamb could distract the store owners while the spider picked the lock? Or they could call in the baa baa black sheep for backup?

I was still laughing as I waved good-bye to Kai and skipped up the steps to Cabin Tranquility.

"Oh good," said Carly when I walked in the door. "At least someone is excited for morning cleanup."

My other cabinmates were standing around the job chart, their bodies droopy. Except for Willa, who had one foot balanced on the edge of the bathroom sink and was bending forward to stretch her arm toward the mirror.

"No one is excited for morning cleanup," whined Bells.

"I hate cleaning," agreed Shira.

"Trust me," said Carly. "Even famous kids need to learn how to clean up after themselves. You never know what life's going to bring."

Carly sighed in a way that made me wonder if she'd been famous when she was younger. Were all the counselors formerly famous? Is that how they got their jobs?

I might have asked, but then I wondered

something else: Did Carly know that I was not famous? Had Joe told her?

I took a step back, as if my secret was suddenly visible. I was grateful when Bells asked, "Were you famous when you were our age, Carly?"

"I was. For a few years I was on a TV singing show with a bunch of other kids. We wore big bows in our hair and did fun dance moves. But then I got older and . . . less sparkly, I guess. It all kind of fizzled out for me."

Willa dropped her foot from the sink and began to do knee bends, her range of movement deepening with every sentence Carly spoke. Carly was still so sparkly. It was hard to imagine anything fizzling out for her.

"Anyway," continued Carly, "I hope you're not trying to distract me. Because nothing is going to stop me from spinning this job chart."

Carly laughed. But unlike her normal laughs, this one seemed forced from her stomach instead of rising from her heart. She tightened her ponytail as she walked over to the job chart.

The job chart was a circle divided into tasks, each task written in silver glitter: toilet, shower, sink, sweeper, and duster. A spinning arrow also lined in glitter was attached to the center. I spun the job of sweeper, which meant I had to sweep the cabin with a broom and dust pan. It wasn't as bad as the bathroom jobs. Bells stood as far from the toilet as possible, looking the other way as she rubbed a brush around the rim. Hazel appeared similarly grossed out by scrubbing the shower.

But none of us complained. We'd somehow come to a silent agreement that making the cabin shine might restore some of Carly's sparkle.

As I swept the floor and then made my bed, I thought about fame. Carly had lost hers. Oliver kept his secret. Hazel didn't want it. Willa seemed worried about losing it. Shira liked that hers was hidden. Bells hinted that she didn't deserve it. And Kai? I didn't know yet how he felt about being famous, but I sensed that it was complicated.

On the airplane I'd thought that fame was something you stepped into, like one of Marin's perfect outfits. Or walked into, like a sleepover with a group of friends and bags of candy.

Maybe being famous was more complicated than I realized. Maybe it wasn't that different from my real life, with good parts like books, vacations to see Grandma, Dad's cheesy jokes, and Mom's reassuring hugs. And also bad parts, like cartwheel disasters, hallway embarrassment, and watching other people group together while I stood alone.

I wondered if Mom had been right when she told me the famous kids would love me just the way I was. I might have more in common with them than I had first thought. Maybe in a few days, after everyone got to know me better, I could confess the truth and they would realize the exact same thing.

But the more I thought about it, the more I brushed the idea away like dirt on the cabin floor. No one liked a liar. Telling the truth was too risky. Especially when I was having so much fun.

Cabin cleanup did seem to restore some of Carly's pep. She was her normal self when she announced that instead of choosing a morning activity, we would be doing something special as a cabin.

"Inscription," said Bells, who was sitting cross-legged on her bed. "We do it on the first morning of camp."

"What's 'inscription'?" asked Willa sharply.

Bells was the princess in the cabin, but Willa had enough spirit in her body to command an army. When Willa lifted her chin, I could practically feel the wind blow. It was easy to understand why she'd been chosen to leap across the movie screen as Clara.

"We decorate our cabin plaque and add our names," explained Hazel. "To make it more, you know, us."

Us. I was part of an us.

We followed Carly onto the porch where she removed the sign that read "Tranquility" and folded the paper in half.

"This boring sign gets replaced with a wooden plaque," explained Carly. "The plaque can be decorated however you want. The only requirement is that it has to include our cabin name and each of your names. But it would be great if it also represented our cabin in some way. My advice is to come up with a plan before you start to paint. Just remember that it's humid out today. The paint is going to take a long time to dry. Try to get it right the first time; otherwise it's going to be a sloppy mess."

"My brother's cabins never planned," said Bells as we walked to the grass field where Carly was setting down a blank plaque. "Every year they just slapped their names around the edge and left it at that."

"When did your brother come to camp?"

"His last summer was five years ago, I think. He came for three summers in a row until he aged out. And every single summer, he won his cabin's plaque. He has one above each of his beds in each of our palaces." Bells leaned down to pick a blade of grass. "That's the way it works with Frederick. He wins everything. Always."

Bells split the blade of grass into two and dropped the shreds to the ground. It was obvious that Bells didn't like talking about her older brother, but there was one thing I had to know. "How did Frederick get the plaque? Doesn't it stay on the cabin?"

Bells shook her head. "On the last day of camp, the counselors slip each cabin plaque into one person's luggage. Like a best camper award. But you only find out if you won it when you get home. Joe doesn't like anyone talking about it, because Camp Famous is supposed to be a break from all that pressure stuff. But everyone who's been here before knows."

A best camper award. Of course. No matter what Joe said, there was no escaping that kids had an order. Most popular to least popular. Smartest to dumbest. Best camper to worst.

As Carly returned carrying a tray of paint and brushes, I imagined what it would feel like to open my duffel bag in three weeks and find the cabin plaque tucked inside.

How would it look hanging above my bed? I desperately wanted to find out.

Carly left to throw the paper away. My cabinmates gathered around the plaque.

The other campers were doing the same in front of their own cabins. Next to us were the girls in Cabin Destiny, all of whom were a year or two older than us. Then came the boys in Cabin Harmony, where Oliver, Cameron Craze, and Kai were staying. Just beyond them were the boys in Cabin Serenity, who were the same age as the girls of Cabin Destiny.

I watched as Oliver dipped his paintbrush into a can of blue paint, examining the bristles before he slowly lowered the brush to his plaque. When Oliver was done, he handed the brush to Kai, who signed his name with just a few strokes, as if he was autographing a large stack of pictures. Cameron Craze shook his head when Kai offered him the brush. He plunged his entire fist into the can of paint, slapping his handprint on the plaque in the place of his name.

Something told me that Cameron Craze would not be finding the Cabin Harmony plaque in his suitcase when he got home.

"Maybe we should measure grid marks before we start to paint," said Shira, bringing my attention back to our plaque. "That way everything will be perfectly even."

"This isn't math class," said Willa. "Not everything has to involve numbers."

"Says the girl who's always counting to herself." Shira did an imitation of Willa raising her arm above her head to a four-count beat. One, two, three, four. One, two, three, four.

"You guys," said Hazel. "Don't fight."

I thought about Carly saying the plaque should represent our cabin. Maybe it should have something to do with the name Tranquility, which I knew from a Ms. McIntyre vocab quiz meant calm. "Twinkle, Twinkle, Little Star" popped into my head. Didn't parents sing that when they wanted their kids to fall asleep?

"What if we do a border of stars?" I suggested. "Like a tranquil night sky."

"That works," said Shira. "But we really should measure if we want to get the stars even."

"Okay," I said. "Shira, you measure. Make dots where we should paint the stars. Then someone could write 'Cabin Tranquility' in the middle, and we can each paint our own names after that."

"Bells has the most beautiful handwriting," said Hazel. "She can do calligraphy. Remember when you tried to teach us last summer?"

"Sort of," said Bells, her voice trailing off.

Of course Bells would have amazing handwriting. That seemed like something a princess would learn from a fancy royal tutor. I smiled at her. "I'd love to see your calligraphy."

"Okay," said Bells. "But only if Shira measures out the letters. She can write them in pencil, and I'll trace over them in paint."

Shira shook her head. "I have the worst handwriting ever. Trust me, you do not want to trace my letters."

"But . . ."

"Come on, Bells," said Hazel. "It'll look so good."

After we all pleaded in unison, even getting down on our knees and clasping our hands in front of us, Bells finally agreed. Shira ran into the cabin to get the ruler that she'd packed along with her protractor and other nonelectronic math supplies. After Shira marked out the stars in pencil, we decided that first Bells should write our cabin name in the center so we could work on the outer rim of the plaque without smudging her letters.

Bells dipped the tip of her brush into the white paint and wiped the bristles until she had a nice point. Her hand shook a bit as she placed the bristles against the wood and began to paint:

Cabin Tra

Bells paused. She refreshed the brush with more paint and continued:

nkwillity

Cabin Trankwillity. Bells looked at our faces and, a few blinks later, realized her mistake. With one quick motion, she swiped her paintbrush through the wet letters and threw it to the ground.

Then she ran off in the direction of the lake.

Shira, Willa, Hazel, and I froze. Our eyes locked on one another, then the plaque, then back to each other.

"Poor Bells," said Hazel. "She's probably so embarrassed. We have to go find her."

"Come on," said Willa. "Quick."

"Wait," I said. "Maybe just one of us is better."

There was a ton at Camp Famous that I did not understand. But embarrassing mistakes? Those I understood. Bells had run off to avoid all of our pity. The last thing she'd want is to be bombarded.

"Abby's right," said Shira.

"I'll go," I volunteered before anyone else could jump in. I didn't know where Bells was, but I wanted to be the one to find her.

I sprinted toward the lake, searching for some trace of the teal T-shirt Bells was wearing. I finally found her a little ways into one of the trails that marked the edge of the forest area. She was hugging her knees to her chest, her back against a tree, as she picked at a mosquito bite on her calf.

I dropped down beside her. "Are you okay?"

"I'm an idiot," she said. "I never should have tried to spell that word."

"Everyone makes spelling mistakes."

"Not like me. I'm lucky if I can spell my own name without messing it up."

"I probably couldn't spell your name either. It's really, really long."

Bells smiled a little as she wiped away a tear that was winding its way down her flushed cheek. "I just hate being so stupid," she said. "At school I have all these extra tutors so no one finds out, and I still barely keep up. It's humiliating. Not that I expect you to understand, since you're a famous writer and all."

No! I wanted to say. I'm not a famous writer. I'm a regular girl who knows exactly how it feels to be humiliated at school. Bells would know that she wasn't alone. That I understood.

But then I remembered the evacuation helicopter—the standard safety precaution to protect the famous kids from anyone who didn't belong at camp. What if Bells panicked and ran to tell Joe that I had lied my way into camp? What if everything was ruined after only one day?

It was a lot to think through as Bells sat, picking her mosquito bite, waiting for a response. With each passing second, I worried it seemed like I was agreeing that I didn't understand. When nothing could be further from the truth.

Then I thought of something. "What about my swim test? Talk about embarrassing." I mimicked myself attempting a freestyle stroke, arms flailing.

Bells laughed. "You weren't that bad."

"I was terrible!"

"Well, it doesn't matter. I'll stay back with you at free swim. The slide gets roasting hot by lunchtime. It's not that great."

"And I'll help you repaint the plaque. Who cares if it's messy? 'Tranquility' is a stupid name anyway."

"I know," said Bells, finally smiling for real. "Who wants to be calm and quiet at camp?"

"Not me," I said.

"Me neither," said Bells. Then she cupped her

hands around her mouth, took a few steps farther into the forest, and screamed as loud as she possibly could.

I did the same. The trees filled with our shouts. Then our laughter. Then a few more shouts.

We kept going until we had nothing left to give.

When everything—our voices, our brains, our hearts—felt clean and empty, we turned back to camp.

We jogged across the grass field, flip-flops smacking. The summer air was warm and heavy against our cheeks, our arms, our legs. As we ran, a thought floated outside of my body like a balloon. It bobbed along in rhythm with our steps, attached to me by a long red string.

I wasn't ready to pull the thought down. Or write it in my notebook. But I liked knowing that I might be able to when the time was right.

The thought was: *Maybe Bells will be my first best friend.*

Dear Notebook,

Sorry about the drops of water. Bells, Shira, and I ran straight from the lake to lunch so my hair is still a little wet. Hopefully it will dry during rest hour.

Free swim was the best! I'd been dreading it since yesterday, when I didn't pass the swim test to use the slide. But Bells stayed back with me and Shira, and we had so much fun. Joe replaced the dead blow-up swans with unicorns. I named my unicorn Majestica, Shira named her unicorn Quantifica, and Bells named hers Bob.

Bells is funny like that. At least, I think she was trying to be funny. But after what happened this morning with the cabin plaque, it also felt sad. Bells has trouble in school, and her parents hire a ton of tutors so that no one finds out. Maybe she chose the name Bob because she was protesting complicated words?

When Bells and I got back from the woods, everyone was waiting for us. They'd tried to wipe off the messed-up word with a paper towel but it was still too wet to paint over. Then Bells remembered that she had a hair dryer in the bottom of one of her trunks. We used it to dry the paint and start from scratch.

The plaque was saved, but when I went back into the cabin to put on my bathing suit, I noticed the picture of Bells's family was gone. I don't know where Bells put it. I think she didn't want her family looking at her anymore.

I wish there was a way I could tell Bells that she's so different from how her family makes her f

Sorry! Bells threw a sock at my head, and I had to throw one back. Do you think Bells knows I was writing about her? There's no way, right? But that's why I still keep you under my bed. People come in and out of our cabin all day long. I don't want to worry about someone looking inside.

I almost forgot to tell you about Shira! I think she's some sort of science genius. She's famous for inventing slime. Her next invention is slime that can burp when it moves. It's top secret right now but maybe she'll send me some when it comes out.

Ah! More sock attacks! Gotta go!

Love,
Abby

I settled into life as a fake famous camper, my
name painted in red letters on the cabin plaque
that we all worked together to fix. Every time I
walked past the plaque—with its perfectly spaced
stars, beautiful cursive letters, the names of my
cabinmates, and the stray blob of blue paint from
when Willa accidentally dropped her paintbrush
in an attempt to swat away a bug—a flicker of joy
sparked inside me.

The plaque was just like Hazel had explained.

It was so *us*.

Every morning when I made my bed and did my cabin chores, I hoped that Carly was taking notice of my neatly folded blankets and the way I scrubbed the toilet without making any gagging noises.

I really wanted to be awarded the cabin plaque.

Sometimes, like during the rare rest hour that we were actually quiet (no flying socks), I imagined Dad hammering a nail into the wall above my bed at home and Mom instructing him to hang the plaque perfectly level. They would be so proud of me. I could almost feel the squeeze of Dad's arms. The brush of Mom's lips against my forehead. In those moments, my small camp bed would feel impossibly large. But then the quiet of rest hour would end, and the fun of camp would begin again.

Every camper was allowed one phone call home, but I never asked permission to use mine. Partly because I knew I couldn't reach my parents. They'd said a gazillion times that they would be out of cell phone range for the entire three weeks.

I could have called Grandma. I had her cell phone number on a piece of scrap paper that I kept inside my notebook. But Grandma had that way of seeing straight into me. Even over the phone, even all the way from Florida, she might ask some question that would lead me to confess that instead of being my regular self, I was pretending to be famous. Grandma would make fitting in seem like a crime.

Besides, before I ever got too homesick, the calm silence of rest hour would be shattered by Willa falling off her bed while doing a complicated stretch, or Shira's slime burping its way across the floor.

The joyful chaos of Camp Famous would resume. I would quickly forget all about missing anyone. And the nights were just as exciting as the days.

One week into camp, we had our first evening campfire. Once the sun went down, we put on our warmest clothes. Bells and I stepped outside the cabin to apply stinky bug spray.

"I'm going to wear this to the next royal ball," said Bells as she pinched her nose and lifted her chin to spray the front of her neck.

"The bug spray?" I asked. "Or that sweatshirt?"

Bells grinned. "I meant the bug spray, but the sweatshirt is a great idea. I'll wear it over a chiffon gown and spritz this smelly stuff on my wrists like perfume. Mother would flip out!"

I laughed as Bells imitated her mother clutching her throat and gasping. "I think even *my* mom would flip out," I said. "And she's not a queen."

Bells lowered her hand. "It must be nice to have a normal mother. Instead of one who's even more famous than you."

"Yeah," I said. "I guess so. I don't really know any different." As always when the subject of fame came up, a warning signal flashed in my brain. I reminded myself to be careful with what I shared.

"Me neither," said Bells. "Do you ever wish you could swap lives with someone? Just for a day. Or a week. Like they do in the movies."

"Yes," I said. "All the time."

"Me too. But then I worry. What if the other person's life was so much better than yours and you had to go back to your old life knowing that it could be different? Like, so much easier." Bells shook her head, as if trying to send the idea away. "Never mind. It's stupid."

"It's not stupid," I said. "It makes perfect sense to me."

Bells rolled her eyes, but her lips raised into a smile. "Thanks, Abby. You're the bestest."

We sat on the front porch of Cabin Tranquility and waited for the rest of our cabin to join. Instead of leaving room for anyone to sit between us, Bells linked her arm in mine, not letting go even when Shira pretended to fall into us. We eventually stuffed all together on the top step, looking into the darkness for the procession of campers led by Joe.

Cabin Tranquility was the last in the row of cabins to be picked up. As the approaching glow of Joe's lit torch glowed bigger and brighter, our normal fizzy energy began to quiet. We settled into a silence that was both warm and soft, like a blanket large enough to wrap around all five of us.

When we joined the end of the line, we held hands and swung our arms in unison as we walked.

The campfire site was at the end of a long path that wound behind the dining hall. Once everyone found a seat on the ground, Joe lowered his torch and lit the stacked wood. Sparks of light burst from the flames.

Bells, who was sitting next to me, leaned over and gave me a quick hug. I hugged her back. The fire was enchanting.

"Welcome, welcome, welcome to our first campfire of the summer, where we join in a tradition that dates back to the founding of Camp Famous eleven years ago." Joe spoke in his normal pattern of three, but his voice was lower than usual. It wove its way between the crackling of the flames. He paced slowly, hands clasped behind his back.

"For thousands of years," he continued,

"humans have gathered around fires to share stories, strengthen communities, and, sometimes, fight off ghosts."

We all scooched closer together. Bells, on my right, grabbed my hand and squeezed. Hazel, on my left, shivered against me. They had both mentioned that campfires were spooky. But they hadn't said anything about ghosts.

Oliver was sitting directly across the fire from me, his knees pulled into his chest. When he noticed me looking, he raised one hand to wave, then returned it to his knees. I waved back, then threaded my hand through Hazel's arm.

"In my pocket," said Joe, "I have some ghost-fighting magic."

Next to Oliver, Cameron Craze made the shape of a gun with both hands and began firing at the flames.

Joe shook his head. "Not that kind of fighting, Cameron. We are fighting our ghosts with a far more powerful weapon—words. Your counselors are coming around with paper and pens. I want you to think about your lives outside of camp. What experiences do you want to leave behind? What haunts you? What whispers in your ear at night?

"It can be anything at all. The scrutiny of being in the public eye, the expectations of those who rely on you, some way that you think you fall short. Whatever it is that you want to be done with, write it down. Then we are going to toss them in the fire and watch them burn, burn, burn."

I slithered my hand free of Bells as a counselor named Ravi handed me a notecard and pen. They were both light as air, but I dropped them to my lap as if they had the weight of bricks. Ever since I'd begun filling the pages of my notebook, writing had come easily. The words flowed from my fingers. But right now I couldn't write as the real me. With other campers so close, I had to write as the famous me in case one of them read my notecard.

What was *she* supposed to write? How did it

feel to have all those eyes on you? To have people rely on you? I had no idea.

All around the campfire, kids were scribbling. Some balanced their notecards on their thighs. Others were hunched over notecards that they'd placed on the ground. Hazel had already flipped her card over to write on the second side.

I glanced at Bells. She tilted her card toward me. It said:

Knowing my brother will always be better than me no matter how hard I try.

I gave Bells a sympathetic smile. I doubted her statement was true, but I was certain that Bells felt that way.

I uncapped my pen. The real me would write that I wanted to burn the feeling of being left out. Set fire to the constant itch inside me that made my eyes skip from one person to the next, wondering what they knew that I didn't.

But that wasn't what Joe meant by "falling short." He meant letting down the people around you who expected great things.

So I wrote the only thing I could think of that also happened to be true:

Sometimes it's hard to know what to write.

Bells leaned over and asked, "What does yours say?"

I showed it to her, tilting the card toward the flame so she could read the words, just like she'd done to me.

"Oh," she said, seeming to read it twice. "I guess that makes sense."

And I couldn't help but wonder if I'd disappointed Bells in some way.

Everyone in my cabin was close, but over the past few days Bells and I had started to find moments when we broke away, just the two of us. Like on the porch with the bug spray. And she'd never once left me at free swim to go on the deep-water slide. Instead, we'd decided that our inflatable unicorns, Majestica and Bob, were madly in love and destined to marry. Shira had agreed that Quantifica would be honored to perform the wedding ceremony.

One rainy afternoon when everyone in our cabin made friendship bracelets out of colorful string, Bells made sure that we did ours in matching colors. She didn't start a new row until she'd confirmed that I was doing the exact same pattern.

As Bells stood up to throw her card in the flames without checking to see if I was coming, I wished that I had written something more on my notecard. Something more *me.* The real me.

Because as my gaze narrowed to Bells's back, I wanted nothing more than to set fire to the way my stomach sank and my skin tingled.

It was the distinct feeling of having messed up.

How I wished I could watch it burn.

After all the cards were thrown into the flame, the edges curling in on themselves as they charred, the spirit of campfire shifted. Joe led us in funny songs. The counselors told stories about knights, dragons, and pesky rabbits. We opened bags of marshmallows and roasted as many as we wanted, our mouths sticky with gooey sweetness.

By the time we returned to Cabin Tranquility, once again following Joe's lit torch, the only tingling I felt was from our fizzy energy. The late hour and the cool chill of night combined to make it bubblier than ever.

Every step of our nighttime routine was more hilarious than any other night so far. Bells placed both feet into one leg of her pajama pants and hopped around the cabin like a rabbit from the campfire story. Shira sang the ABC's as she gurgled mouthwash, almost choking and spewing it all over the sink. Willa started spinning pirouettes in the center of the cabin. Hazel jumped into my bed and I jumped into her bed.

And Carly? She stood in the doorway, hands on her hips, shaking her head and trying hard not to laugh.

When we finally got into our beds (the correct beds), it was hard to stop wiggling and jiggling. Bells started a whisper chain so that once Carly fell asleep we could keep talking. The sooner we quieted down, the sooner Carly would pull her pink satin sleep mask over her eyes and fall asleep.

Carly's counselor bed was in a corner nook tucked behind a half wall. Willa was the only one who could see into Carly's space from her own bed. When Willa gave a thumbs-up signal, we all crept over to Bells's bed.

We'd never formally decided that Bells's bed would be the gathering place. When there were things to be discussed, like whether Cameron Craze was aware that he was constantly jerking his body around or if his elbow jabs were unconscious dance moves that everyone in the world would soon be copying, we discussed them on Bells's bed.

I usually sat right beside Bells, my back against her pillow. But after what happened at the campfire, I paused to make sure she wanted me there. When Bells patted the spot beside her, I snuggled in with relief. Bells's bed smelled like lavender and bug spray. I brushed my hand against her super-soft cashmere blanket and smiled.

"I love camp," said Shira. "I never want it to end."

"Me neither," said Bells. "Let's mount a rebellion and refuse to leave. I could live like this forever."

"We can't live like this forever," said Willa. "Those stupid notecards made me remember all those other people."

In the past week, Willa had cut down on her dance exercises against the bathroom sink, and she hadn't mentioned the movie script since the day we arrived. Now she waved her graceful hands in the air, giving the impression of a large crowd waiting just outside the cabin door.

If I never left camp, my parents would miss me. So would Grandma. Ms. McIntyre would send a nice check-in letter, but the kids at school would forget about me pretty darn fast.

Except everyone else seemed to agree with Willa.

"People," repeated Hazel. "I hate people. I hate how they think they know everything about me just because they read what my mom writes. You guys are the only ones who really know me."

"Same," said Bells. "I'm dreading that look. You

know, the one where someone meets you and at first they're really excited. But then you can tell that they're also disappointed. Like they expected you to be prettier."

"Or smarter," said Shira.

"Or more outgoing," said Hazel.

"The famous version of you," said Bells.

Again, everyone agreed. I twisted the corner of Bells's blanket between my fingers.

"At least when I'm dancing, I'm the real me," said Willa. "I'm probably the most me, if that makes sense."

Yes, I thought. Finally something I could relate to. "That's how I feel when I'm writing," I said.

Willa smiled. "We're lucky, I guess. We're famous for doing what we love."

Just like at the campfire, my words were true. When I wrote in my notebook, I was the most me. The outside world lifted from my shoulders, and my thoughts untangled without any worry of what others would think, or say, or do.

But what my words *implied* was false. My cabinmates assumed I was referring to all my famous books.

"Do you ever write about romance?" asked Bells, shaking her shoulders. "Like kissing and stuff?"

Did the fake famous me write about kissing? How could I? I'd never been close to kissing anyone in a romantic way.

"Come on, Abby," pressed Bells. "Tell us. You spend every rest hour writing, but you never talk about your books. We don't even know what they're about."

Bells assumed I was writing stories during rest hour. What would she think if she knew I was just writing about my thoughts and feelings?

"Yeah," said Willa. "You're so secretive, Abby. You never tell us anything."

"I'm not allowed to," I said. "It's, like, against the rules."

Shira rolled her eyes and blew air out of the side of her mouth. "You mean because you signed a contract? That legal stuff doesn't matter. It's just us."

I looked around at my friend's faces, lit up by a single flashlight. They all seemed to agree that legal stuff—whatever that meant—didn't matter.

Or maybe they were all agreeing that I was being secretive. Since the minute I'd made my decision on the airplane, I *had* been keeping a secret. A big secret.

I had to tell them something.

"Sometimes I write about crushes and stuff," I lied. "But only kissing. Nothing else."

"Like, what do you write?" asked Bells. "Do you describe it?" Bells tilted her head and puckered her lips.

"I mean . . . yeah . . . I just sort of write that my characters kissed and that they felt happy. That kind of thing."

"Happy?" said Willa. "Don't you mean that their hearts exploded?"

"And then they kissed again," added Hazel. "And again and again and again."

"Oooh," said Shira, wrapping her arms around herself and wiggling. "Romantic."

I grabbed one of Bells's pillows and threw it at Shira. Hazel did the same. Shira rolled off the bed and landed on the wood floor with a thump.

"I'm dead," said Shira as she threw her hand across her forehead and pretended to gasp for air. "And I haven't even had my first kiss."

We all laughed, which is why we missed the creak of Carly's bed frame.

"Girls," said Carly, sitting up and lifting her pink satin eye mask. "Get back in your own beds and go to sleep. Or else."

We scattered back to our own beds.

I pulled my sheets to my chin as stray giggles echoed around the cabin. I'd survived their questions about my writing, but just barely.

Normally I never wanted our nighttime conversations to end. But that night I was grateful when the giggles stopped.

For the first time since arriving at Camp Famous, I preferred silence to talking.

After that night, I made more of an effort to talk about my (fake) famous life outside of camp. My cabinmates had begun to glance at me when they were talking about magazines that had written mean things about them, or the adults who forced them to attend meetings when they really wanted to stay home and watch YouTube videos.

They seemed to be keeping closer track of when I did, or did not, join the conversation.

I had figured out by then that part of being famous was being the center of attention, and also not having control. So when Cameron Craze complained one day at lunch about a producer who made him miss his best friend's birthday party because they needed new content for his dance videos, I said the same thing had happened to me when I was behind schedule on a book.

When Hazel shared that she'd once been followed home from school by a fan of her mom's blog who wanted her to pose for a picture, I told a story about the time a reader threw a book at my face because she hated the sad ending.

The lies burned as they left my mouth. I'd lose track of the rest of the conversation because they swirled in my head like loud angry insects.

But after a few days, the pressure eased. My friends no longer seemed to wait for my contribution to conversations about fame.

I could go back to being a closer version of the real me.

One morning toward the end of the second week of camp, when Bells suggested that our entire cabin sign up for canoeing, I happily agreed.

Canoeing wasn't very popular. But Shira and Hazel had done it the day before, and they'd seen a family of baby turtles in a patch of water lilies. Shira said one of them had climbed into her palm.

Who wouldn't want to hold a baby turtle?

My whole cabin raised our hands for canoeing at morning circle. Kai, who was sitting next to me, raised his hand as well, even though he'd said at breakfast that he was probably going to sign up for fire building.

"Did you hear about the baby turtles?" I asked him.

"No. But I'm stuck on this song ending. At first I thought staring into flames might help me figure it out, but maybe being on the lake is a better idea. Or maybe I just stink at writing lyrics and nothing will help."

Kai hadn't shared any of his songs with me. I'd noticed him singing yesterday on the way to the dining hall, but he stopped when I got close enough to make out his words. "What's the song about?" I asked.

"It's about everything that I don't know. So it's pretty long. And pretty pathetic." Kai fake laughed at his words. So I did as well. He cleared his bangs from his eyes, and I noticed his nails were chewed. The skin around the edges ragged.

I was tempted to tell Kai there was no way his list of unknowns was as long as my list. And also—how much I loved the song idea. Kids who followed his music would be grateful to hear that even *Kai Carter* didn't understand a lot about life. Except my friendship with Kai was different from my friendship with Bells and the other girls in my cabin. Kai was fun to joke around with, but I wasn't sure if it would be weird to get all deep and serious with him. I came up with something in the middle.

"Maybe split your list up into different songs?" I suggested. "Think about the nursery rhymes. They're short because they're for little kids, but maybe that's also why you never forget them. Because they're simple and easy to understand. You know, like the itsy-bitsy spider reminds you to get back up and try again. No matter what."

Kai nodded. "That's actually totally helpful. Keep it simple. Each unknown thing could be its own song. That would definitely fill a whole album. Thanks, Abby."

Had I just helped Kai Carter figure out his next album?

I sat up a little taller on the wooden bench as sign-ups continued. Cameron Craze also raised his hand for canoeing. Oliver signed up for a nature hike. We were about to break into activity groups when Joe tapped me on the shoulder.

"Abby," said Joe. "Quick word?"

I'd been purposefully avoiding Joe, limiting our interactions to quick smiles and fast waves. Every time he caught my eye, I tried to make it clear with my expression that I was totally fine, totally okay, totally happy to be at Camp Famous. There was no need to check on me or acknowledge our real-life connection to Ms. McIntyre—my teacher, his sister.

I assumed that Joe knew by then that I was claiming to be a famous writer. And I didn't want to know what he felt about that.

Now I had no choice. I followed Joe a few steps away from the meeting circle, where he crouched down so his face was level with mine and said, "So so *so* sorry to tell you this, Abby. But you can't take out a canoe until you pass the deep-water test."

"What? Are you sure?"

Shira had gone canoeing the day before, and she hadn't passed the deep-water test either.

"Completely sure," said Joe. "Camp rules. No messing around with water safety. I apologize if I didn't make that clear from the get-go."

I thought back to the swim test on the first day of camp. Shira and I had been talking. Then we'd stepped back to be last in line. I must have missed Joe explaining about the canoes. After all, the test was called the deep-water test, not the slide test.

"But . . . Shira."

I didn't want to tell on Shira, but I also didn't know how Joe had let her go out in a canoe. He was at almost every morning and afternoon circle, watching to see who signed up for what, encouraging kids to try new activities. How had Shira slipped by?

"Shira passed her deep-water test two days ago," said Joe. "And you're welcome to try again, anytime. Just let me know and I'll definitely, definitely, *definitely* make it happen."

I looked over Joe's shoulder to where Shira stood next to Bells. Shira was trying to get Bells's attention, probably telling her that they needed to go back to the cabin to change into bathing suits. Bells motioned that she was waiting for me.

How could I tell them that I was the only one who wasn't allowed to go?

Joe read my mind. "Your friends don't care about a swim test, Abby. They like you because of who you are on the inside. That's all that matters."

If that was true, then why didn't Shira tell me she was retaking the deep-water test? Why keep it a secret?

Joe reminded me of Mom. He spoke with confidence, but something didn't connect. This was about more than a swim test. It was about once again being on the outside.

Shira placed her hand on Bells's arm and leaned over to whisper in her ear. Shira's cupped hand reminded me of Quinn whispering to Marin. My body was standing beside the meeting circle at Camp Famous, but my heart felt like it was back at school.

It ached in a very familiar way.

Except this time, Bells listened to what Shira had to say and then came right over to me.

"Abby," she said. "I just heard about the swim test. Do you want me to pick a different activity with you? I don't care about baby turtles. They're slow. And smelly. I mean, they're probably smelly, right?"

I smiled. Bells was trying. But I shook my head. "No. You should go."

"I don't want to go without you. Should we switch to yoga? My mother loves yoga."

"That's because all old people love yoga."

I tried to keep my voice light. Bells had passed the swim test easily. I didn't want to say out loud how embarrassing it was to now be the only kid in the entire camp who hadn't passed.

"Seriously," I said. "It's just morning activity. I'll go on the nature hike with Oliver and meet you at the lake for free swim. Majestica and Bob can reunite in true love."

"Are you sure?"

I nodded. "I'm sure."

I tried to appear brave. To smile like I had wanted to go on a nature hike all along. When Shira waved an apologetic wave, seeming to mouth *sorry,* I shrugged like it was no big deal.

Oliver appeared beside me. "Did you say you're joining the nature hike, Abby? You're going to love it. I'll show you the best lookout spot in all of camp. It's this enormous rock with slits on the side that look just like real stairs. We'll probably be able to see all our friends canoeing in the lake. Maybe we can yell super loud and pretend to be forest ghosts." Oliver made a ghostly sound. "Oooh—I see you down there."

As Oliver skipped over to Ravi, the counselor who was leading the nature hike, I thought about his words—"all our friends."

Oliver was friends with everyone at Camp Famous. I'd seen him sprint across the field to the tetherball court with a rock climber named Charlie. They played round after round of the game during free time. He sat next to Kai at most meeting circles, where they would crack up over whispered jokes. Last night after dinner, Cameron Craze and Oliver led the whole camp in learning a new dance that Cameron said was inspired by "my bud Oliver."

The dance was called the clunky robot. Cameron was sure it would be his next viral hit.

And yet, Oliver was the same boy as at school. He had the same habit of raising his pointer finger before he spoke, as if a lightbulb had just gone off in his brain. He had the same rushed way of talking, his words pouring out of his mouth like shaken soda exploding from a can.

How did he do it? How did Oliver not care that he was the only one who had signed up for the nature hike while I was on the verge of tears watching Bells and Shira walk away without me? How did Oliver maintain the peppy cheerfulness of Carly and the steady determination of Joe?

How was he so himself all the time?

As we followed Ravi toward a narrow dirt path that ran into the woods, Oliver skipping a few steps ahead of me, I realized that ever since we'd arrived at Camp Famous, I'd been treating Oliver like a truth bomb in boy form. As if one wrong word from him would blow my entire camp experience into flames. I scooted away from him at meals. I gave him nervous glances whenever he told stories about home. Or school. *Our* school.

Now that we were alone, my body relaxed a bit with relief. Not just because I didn't have to worry about whether Oliver would blow my cover, but because I could talk to Oliver as real Abby, not famous Abby. I waited until we entered an area thick with evergreen trees. Ravi walked a few steps ahead, searching the growth around the edge of the path for four-leaf clovers.

"Oliver," I said. "Thanks for not telling anyone about me."

"Of course, Abby. I'm a secret-keeping expert." He ran his fingers along his lips, as if he was zipping them shut. "You can trust me," he mumbled with his mouth shut tight. "I'll never tell anyone."

We talked about camp as we walked deeper into the woods: how good the food was, how fun the activities were. When I mentioned how much better the air smelled at camp than at home, it opened the door to talking about school.

Oliver did an amazing impersonation of the way Quinn would react if she knew I had become friends with Kai Carter. He let his jaw drop and extended his hands to his side, his fingers splayed. He looked left, then right, then left again. It reminded me of Cameron Craze's clunky robot dance.

Who knew Oliver Frank was so funny?

When I finally stopped laughing I asked, "Is it hard to lie about Camp Famous at school?"

"I never lie," said Oliver. "I've told people at school that I know Kai and Bells and Cameron Craze. It's not my fault that no one cares."

"You never told me—" I paused. A memory of the school hallway popped into my head. The day of my parents' mysterious meeting with Ms. McIntyre. Marin and Quinn were talking about Kai Carter and Oliver had said, loud and clear, that he knew Kai Carter.

And no one thought for a single second that Oliver actually *knew* Kai Carter.

"So why do you write your articles under the name Francis Oliver? Why can't you use your real name and just be one person? Then maybe kids at school would, you know, care more." I paused. "Maybe they'd like you more."

"My parents insisted that I write under a different name to protect my privacy. At least until I'm eighteen. And I don't want kids to like me because I'm famous, Abby. I want them to like me just the way I am."

That was it. The reason Oliver was himself all the time was because he didn't want to be anyone else. He was proud to be Oliver Frank.

I wondered if I could ever feel that way, too.

"Oliver, do you think I'm different here than at school?"

Oliver stopped walking. He turned to face me. There was a Grandma-ish look in his eyes, as if he was looking deep into me. Ravi was a few feet behind us, still lost in his search for good-luck clovers. I was tempted to run over and join him.

Anything to take Oliver's eyes off me.

Then Oliver shook his head. "No, Abby," he said. "I think you're pretty much exactly the same."

We continued on in silence, Oliver's answer echoing in my ears. Was I pretty much the same? If so, was that a good thing?

Part of the reason I'd wanted to go to Camp Longatocket was to figure out if I had trouble making friends at school because of bad luck or because something was wrong with me. I wanted to start fresh with a whole new group of kids who knew nothing about me and see what happened.

In the swirl of winding up at Camp Famous, I'd thought lying about my true self was my best option. But if that lie hadn't changed how I acted, did it matter? Would Bells and Kai and everyone else like the regular me?

I wished there was a way to know for sure.

Then maybe I'd also figure out why Shira hadn't told me about the swim test. Because as Oliver and I climbed onto his favorite rock, we could see Shira and Bells laughing together as they paddled a canoe. They were splashing Kai and Cameron with the flat part of their oars.

The questions that arose inside me as I watched—about what Shira thought about me, what I might have done wrong to make her feel that way—were the exact same ones that haunted me in my regular life. Oliver had said we could sit on the rock and pretend to be forest ghosts. I hadn't realized that my real-life worries would be the scariest of all.

They were deep inside me. Trapped. And I had no idea how to make them go away.

Dear Notebook,

I've got happy news and sad news. I don't know which to tell you first.

I guess I'll start with happy. It's easier. My happy news is that Kai told me his songs are finally working. And he's going to change the name of his upcoming world tour from "The Heartbreak Express" to "Down Came the Rain." He doesn't care what his managers say. It's his name on all the albums, so he's going to start deciding what to sing in them. Then he said that our game inspired him.

So, hooray! I inspired a pop star!

I wish that was all I had to report. But something else happened today. I finally figured out why Shira retook her swim test without telling me. Shira told Willa that Bells and I were excluding her during free swim. She said we hurt her feelings by always pretending that our unicorns were in love and that Shira's unicorn would be the one to perform the ceremony. So one day when Willa and Shira said they were going to the Art Hut to make mosaic frames, they actually went to the lake, where Shira retook her test.

Carly made our whole cabin sit in a circle and talk it out. Shira explained how she always feels left out at home because she's in all these advanced college chemistry classes and that she didn't want Quantifica to feel left out. She said that even though she knew we weren't doing it on purpose, she hated feeling that way at camp.

I know how it feels to be left out, but I had no idea how it felt to be the person who excluded someone else. When Shira explained her side of things, I almost started to cry. I felt terrible! I apologized a million times, and Shira said it was okay. She forgives me. But I'm not sure I forgive myself. Not all the way.

I wonder if this will hurt my chances of getting the cabin plaque? Sorry, Notebook. I know I shouldn't be thinking about that right now. I really am sorry about Shira.

Abby

A few days later Joe stood up at lunch and tapped his glass with the edge of his knife. "All right, all right, all right," he said. "It's another beautiful day here at camp. We've got one important schedule change for the afternoon."

Schedule changes were a good thing. They meant afternoon ice cream sundae bars in the dining hall, movie nights on the center field, a day off from cabin chores.

Bells leaned over and whispered to me, "Probably cabin skit night."

I didn't know what that involved, but it sounded fun.

I turned to Shira, who was sitting on the other side of me, and repeated the news to her, even though she'd been to Camp Famous before and probably already knew. Ever since our cabin meeting with Carly, I'd been making an extra effort to include Shira in everything. It seemed to be working. Shira smiled at me and wiggled her shoulders in excitement.

"Instead of afternoon activity," continued Joe, "you'll meet as a cabin to start planning your performance for skit night, which is Friday night, just five days away. For our new campers, skit night is a time for your cabin to get up on stage and show us what you've got. I want to be clear that this is not a competition. There are no winners and there are no losers here at Camp Famous. This is just a time to celebrate the end of camp with lots of fun, fun, fun."

There it was. The first official reminder that camp would be ending soon.

Camp days had nothing in common with regular days. There were no quizzes or assemblies or PE classes that required remembering sneakers to mark one day from the next. But I'd arrived at camp on a Saturday, which meant camp ended on a Saturday.

Joe sat down. The clanging of forks and spoons replaced his words. But I was suddenly not hungry.

"It's not entirely true," said Bells as she took a sip of water.

"What's not?"

"The whole winners and losers part. The counselors won't admit it, but according to my brother, if they're undecided about who should get the cabin plaque, they give it to the person who comes up with the skit idea. Frederick came up with his cabin's idea every year. Obviously."

I'd been wondering how Carly was going to choose. None of us were perfect. Shira complained the most about chores, but Willa's space was the messiest. Hazel was forgetful and always late to things. Bells and I had hurt Shira's feelings.

If coming up with a skit idea would push me closer to going home with the plaque, then I was going to give it my best shot.

"Can the skits be about anything?" I asked.

Bells nodded. "As long as they have to do with our cabin."

My brain began to spin. How long were the skits? What were they usually about? Did we need costumes? Songs? Jokes?

"Don't worry," said Bells, as if reading my mind. "I already have some really good ideas."

At rest hour, instead of writing about my day in my notebook, I tried to think of ideas. When nothing came to mind, I began to read through all my old entries. By the time Carly called an end to rest hour and we gathered as a cabin on the porch, I still didn't have anything good.

Neither, it turns out, did anyone else.

"We could do a winter-in-summer theme and

be snowflakes," said Willa. "I could choreograph the perfect dance for us."

"Or we could pretend to be molecules with a magnetic pull," said Shira. "Something that shows we're stronger together than we are apart."

"I don't know," said Hazel. "Winter seems . . . brrr. And I'm sorry, Shira, but I have no idea what you're talking about."

"Think about your strong friendships, girls," suggested Carly. "That's what Cabin Tranquility is all about. That's what we need to show to the rest of the camp."

How do you show strong friendships? I knew how kids did it at school. With matching jewelry and playdates . . . an idea popped into my head!

I thought about the day when Quinn had brought her Polaroid camera to school. Quinn, Marin, and all their popular friends had posed on the front lawn of school, taking a whole roll of film in barely ten minutes. As each picture dropped from the camera, Quinn handed out the images to her friends. Every girl with a picture slid the photograph into the plastic cover of her school binder.

They kept them there all year long. Sometimes they would trace the white edges of the Polaroid picture with their fingers. Other times they would seem to forget about the pictures entirely.

I never forgot. Every single school day, I was reminded of not being invited to join.

"Maybe we could be the pictures inside a Polaroid camera," I suggested. "We can make a big picture frame out of cardboard and paint it white. We could act out scenes of all the things we like to do together. It'll show that we want to remember our friendship forever, like a picture."

"I like that," said Shira.

"Me too," said Willa.

Neither Hazel nor Bells said anything. Hazel continued scratching her fingernail into the wood floor, and Bells fiddled with the edge of her shorts.

But every other idea had immediately been

dismissed, so I took their silence as a good sign. I even glanced up at the cabin plaque, imagining it hanging over my bed at home.

Then Bells said, "I have another idea." She'd already suggested three, and now she wanted to take a song from a musical that no one else had seen and change the words to use memories from camp. "I guarantee everyone will have our cabin's song stuck in their head for the rest of the summer. The musical is only in previews. It's very exclusive."

Bells began to hum the song. It was catchy. It was also clear that Bells kept losing the beat a few lines in. I wanted to point out that Bells's idea would mean somehow finding the real words, learning the actual beat, and then coming up with an entire new song. How would we do that when there were no electronics allowed at camp?

Except that Bells wanted to win the plaque just as much as I did. Objecting to her idea would risk hurting her feelings, which is why I'd kept quiet when she'd proposed her other ideas. But saying nothing would risk losing the cabin plaque. I thought back to all the conversations about fame that I'd heard over the past two weeks. A lot of them involved taking pictures.

"You know," I said, "we always say it's annoying that everyone thinks they know us just because they see our pictures everywhere."

Shira cleared her throat like a grown-up.

"I mean, not me and Shira, obviously," I continued. "But Hazel, your mom takes pictures of you all day long and shares them without your permission. And Willa, the worst part of your movie audition was when that photographer took photos of you so the director could decide if he liked the way you'd look on a poster. And Bells, what about the royal ceremonies where you have stand like a statue for hours while people wait in line to pose with your family? My skit idea uses pictures for a good reason. To show who we really are."

Hazel stopped scratching the wood, and Willa nodded in agreement. I sensed they were with me.

Maybe there was something more I could say to convince Bells and Shira?

I had to think fast. This was my chance.

"I wrote a book about this, actually. It was about a group of popular girls and every morning they took a picture with all their popular friends. And if you weren't in the morning picture, you weren't allowed to hang out with them. There was this one girl whose feelings got really hurt. And yeah, the story kind of went on from there with revenge and all that."

"What happened?" asked Shira, leaning toward me. "How did she get her revenge?"

"Oh, she formed a group with some other left-out girls. I can't say too much. The book hasn't been published yet. It's coming out after I get home."

I bit my lip. Maybe it seemed like I was letting the words sink in, but I was actually trying to stop talking. I had no idea how that girl got revenge! If I had known, maybe I would have tried to do something similar in real life.

"Please tell me it involves either vampires, werewolves, or zombies," said Shira. "Any of them will do."

I squeezed out a forced laugh. "You'll have to read the book to find out."

Bells squinted her eyes. "I don't know if people will get it, Abby. Especially since the book hasn't come out yet. And what do pictures have to do with zombies getting revenge?"

I had begun to explain that there were no zombies in this particular book when Carly stopped me. "Come on, girls, we're getting offtrack. This skit is supposed to bring us together, not tear us apart. Why don't we combine the two ideas? We can sing Bells's song from inside Abby's picture frame. What do you guys think? The best of both worlds, right?"

The rhythmic pounding of the tetherball and the sound of splashing from the lake broke our silence. The other cabins had already decided their skits and were free to enjoy their afternoon.

"Good idea," said Willa, jumping to stand. "Now can we go swimming? I'm roasting."

"Broiling," agreed Shira.

"Melting," added Hazel.

"Yes," said Carly with a clap. "Sounds like we have a decision. That's enough skit talk for one day. Let's all go down to the lake to cool off, okay?"

Was it a decision? I wasn't sure. Carly acted as though she had clapped all the tension away. But I could still feel it floating in the air like dust mites—nearly invisible, but also everywhere. No one spoke as we changed into our bathing suits. Bells left the cabin with Shira, her towel draped over her arm. Hazel, Willa, and I followed behind.

The split made sense. This part of the path wasn't wide enough for five girls to walk side by side.

But as I watched Bells from behind, her head tilted toward Willa, my heart lurched like Shira's burping slime.

"Do you think Bells is mad at me?" I asked Hazel and Shira.

"She shouldn't be," said Hazel.

"We're doing both your ideas," said Shira. "And anyway, who cares?"

Shira had a point. We were doing both our skit ideas. So technically both of us had won. Neither of us had lost. That was good, right?

When we reached the lake, I draped my towel over the fence, just like always. I followed my friends onto the dock. We walked in a row: Willa, then Shira, then Bells, then Hazel, then me. Willa grabbed Shira's hand. They walked to the far end of the dock, counted to three, and dove into the deep water to swim out to the slide. Hazel called for them to wait up and dove in after them.

It had been so many free swims. So many hours spent floating on Majestica and Bob. So many falls off their slippery plastic backs and so many failed attempts to climb back on. So many conversations. So much laughter.

I assumed Bells would stay back with me.

But Bells kept walking, not even glancing back at me as she raised up on her toes, sprang into a perfect dive, and stroked toward the deep-water slide.

As she swam, my hopes for a best friend went with her. Both of them too far away to reach.

I tried to make things better with Bells at the lake. I didn't ride Majestica. I sat on the dock, my lower legs swaying in the water, and waited for my friends to return from the slide.

I tried in the cabin. When Bells and I both walked to the door to hang our towels on the clothesline, I stepped aside so Bells could go first. I waited on the porch until she was done, then I hung my towel all scrunched up so that hers could lay flat and dry faster.

When Kai asked if I could listen to a new song

idea, I made sure Bells didn't see us walking across the field together.

I tried that night at evening activity. When Cameron Craze asked me to be his partner for a game where you had to follow your partner's hand signals, I told him he should ask Bells instead. No one was better at movement games than Cameron.

I made myself small in the hopes that Bells would eventually forget her anger. As if she would wake up tomorrow morning like a fairy-tale princess who'd been under a sleeping spell, blinking her eyes to a world in which we were friends again.

But trying that hard was . . . hard. My mind was always two steps ahead of my body, evaluating my actions and how they would look through Bells's eyes.

Even writing in my notebook at rest hour the next day didn't help. I couldn't find the right words to put on the page. When I wrote that I was mad at myself for lying to get my skit chosen, in the next sentence I wrote that I was mad at Bells for being such a baby.

I was wrong. She was wrong.

I should apologize. She should apologize.

I should move on. She should move on.

I deserved the cabin plaque. She deserved the cabin plaque.

Normally writing helped me make sense of things. But what if writing was no longer enough? What if I was in too deep? What if this time I needed to say actual words out loud to someone who would listen and offer their own words in return?

I still had my one phone call. But how could I begin to explain this mess to Grandma? Where would I start? With my fake fame? My friendship with an actual princess? My wrecking ball of a mistake?

No. Grandma was far away in sunny Florida. She would be playing card games with her friends, maybe sipping her favorite chilled tomato juice with a squeeze of lemon. By the time I explained everything, her tomato juice would be warm and I'd be late for afternoon circle. It would be just like at school when my parents went in for their top secret meeting with Ms. McIntyre. Everyone would notice my late arrival and wonder what was wrong.

I needed to talk to someone who was here. Someone who understood the importance of cabin skit night. Someone who understood how I hadn't meant to mess everything up; it was just what happened to people like me.

The *real* me.

There was only one person who checked all those boxes: Oliver Frank.

When rest hour ended, I ran right to afternoon circle, hoping to find Oliver alone. But by the time I arrived, he was already wedged in between Charlie the rock climber and Cameron Craze.

My next thought was to sign up for whatever activity Oliver raised his hand for. Maybe if he chose something popular, like pottery in the Art Hut or fire building at the campfire site, I'd be able to pull him away for a few minutes of private conversation without anyone noticing.

When Oliver raised his hand for meditation in the Zendom with Joe, I didn't know what to do. No one ever signed up for meditation. Hazel's early warnings about Joe's smelly feet had proven true.

In desperation, I smiled at Bells once more. Maybe, just maybe, she'd forgive me. When Bells looked at the dirt beneath her feet instead of returning my smile, I realized it was meditation with Oliver or the silent treatment from Bells.

They both involved quiet. But only one made my heart ache with worry.

I raised my hand for meditation.

"Pssst, Oliver," I whispered half an hour later.

We were sitting on maroon cushions in the Zendom. Joe sat at the front of the room, his posture perfect, his eyes closed. A recording of waterfalls played in an endless loop. It was like being trapped inside a ball of static. Oliver and I could sneak out and Joe would never know.

"Please," I tried again. "It's important." I flicked Oliver on the shoulder.

He opened his eyes. Finally. "What?"

"I need to talk to you."

I rolled off my cushion and crawled across the wooden floor. I pushed on the door and propped it open with the flip-flop that I'd left outside. Joe didn't even flinch.

Oliver, on the other hand, could not decide what to do. He looked from me to Joe. Joe to me. Finally he rolled off his cushion and crawled to join me outside.

"What's going on, Abby?"

His eyes bulged, as if maybe someone had gotten hurt. What if I was making too big a deal out of this? What if Oliver couldn't understand?

"Bells is mad at me," I said.

"How come?"

It was so tempting to pretend like I didn't know. I wanted sympathy. I wanted someone to take my side. To tell me that it would all be okay.

But even more than that, I wanted to tell someone the truth. So I did. As Joe breathed in and breathed out, I told Oliver the whole cabin skit story.

When I finished, the first thing Oliver said was, "Someone should tell Shira that vampires, werewolves, *and* zombies are too much for one book. No one would ever believe it would take that many creatures to get revenge on the popular girls."

"That's not the point, Oliver."

"Still, Shira deserves to know."

I sighed and rolled my eyes. "Fine. I'll tell her right after I also confess that I'm not actually a famous writer. That I'm just a totally regular kid."

"Sounds good," said Oliver. He turned as if he was going to walk back into the Zendom.

"Wait! I was kidding! Of course I'm not going to tell anyone any of that."

"Why not? It would probably make everything better."

I began to object. There were only a few days left

of camp. I'd made it this far. Why ruin everything?

Except all my excuses lodged in my throat like an enormous gumball. They would buy me time, but sooner or later Bells was bound to find out the truth about me. Would admitting it first make everything better?

"Famous kids are used to dealing with adults," said Oliver. "They're good at knowing when people aren't telling them the whole story."

"So you think Bells knows?"

"I think she's starting to wonder," said Oliver. "And I think you are, too. Maybe it's time to tell the truth."

I walked back to Cabin Tranquility deep in thought. Oliver was right. I had to tell Bells, and the rest of my cabinmates, the truth. It was time.

In my head I rehearsed what I was going to say and how I was going to say it. I would explain how fast everything had happened. How I hadn't meant to cause any harm, just make friends. Bells would be hugging me in no time. They all would.

But then I pushed open the screen door. And froze.

The scene inside Cabin Tranquility came to me

in pieces, like separate photographs.

Bells, Hazel, Shira, and Willa all gathered on my bed.

My notebook open on Bells's lap.

Their faces peering down at an open page filled with my handwriting in blue ink.

I was too shocked to reach for my notebook. "What are you doing?" was the only thing I could manage to say.

Bells looked up. She closed the notebook and placed both hands flat on the cover. "Nothing," she said. "Just reading. Isn't that what you want people to do, Abby? Read what you write?"

Although Bells hardly moved, Hazel, Shira, and Willa stood up. The bed creaked with their shifting weight.

"That's my private notebook."

"Well," said Bells, moving the notebook from her lap to the bed. "It's funny that you should mention privacy. We know what you've been up to."

"Up to? What are you talking about?"

Shira leaned forward as if she was going to interrupt. But Bells shook her head and continued. "We've all seen you scribbling away at rest hour. At first we thought you were just writing personal stuff in a journal, or maybe your next book. But you were so secretive about your work that we started to wonder what you were actually writing. And now we know. Are you a spy, Abby? Is that why you're here? To sell our secrets to the tabloids?"

I had to separate Bells's words to make sense of their meaning.

"A spy"—someone who pretends to be part of a group that they don't belong to.

"The tabloids"—magazines like the ones I'd seen in the grocery store full of scandalous stories about celebrities.

Bells thought I'd been taking notes about everyone at camp so that I could share them with the world. What had Bells read? How many pages?

I lunged for my notebook, hugging it to my chest. "How could you do this to me? You took this from my backpack under my bed."

"How could *we* do this to *you*? How could *you* do this to *us*? Besides, we only glanced at one page. But it was enough to confirm what I'd long suspected. Kai Carter's tour name? Seriously, Abby. What were you planning on doing? Splashing the name change on the front page of every magazine?"

They'd read the page where I wrote about the Down Came the Rain tour. I couldn't decide if that was better or worse than reading the pages from before camp.

"You don't understand," I said.

"Actually, I'm quite certain that we do."

"Hold on," said Shira. "Give Abby a chance to explain. I'm sure it's all just a big misunderstanding. Right, Abby?"

Shira nodded at me, as if she was eager to write down my explanation and solve it like a math problem. Hazel had a similarly hopeful expression.

Willa was more difficult to read. Her arms

were crossed, and her face had the same focused concentration as when she did her dance exercises.

"Go ahead," said Bells, with a lift of her chin. "Prove it."

Yes. I could prove it. I had the words all ready.

"I'm not a famous writer," I said. "I'm not a famous anything. I'm just a totally regular kid who didn't even know she was coming to Camp Famous until I got to the airport. I lied about being famous so I would fit in. Not to sell stories to a tabloid. I'm not even allowed to buy tabloids. I would have no idea how—"

"So you admit you're a liar, Abby," interrupted Bells. "I mean, assuming that's your real name."

"It is. My name's Abby. Abigail Jane Herman. I'm telling the truth. I swear."

"I don't know," said Hazel, taking a nervous step away from me, her hair falling in front of her face like a shield. "Something doesn't feel right."

"I'm not a spy, I promise. Look. You can read my entire notebook. Read the first pages. I wrote them when I was still at school. My totally regular school."

Bells huffed. "Right. Like that proves anything. We all know how sneaky reporters are. Of course you had a whole story ready in case you got caught."

"Ask Oliver," I said, convinced I'd found the perfect solution. "We go to school together. He'll tell you."

"Isn't Oliver a reporter, too?" asked Willa, looking to the others for confirmation. "You guys probably work together. Nice try, Abby."

Willa said my name as if it was in quotations. As if it was fake.

"What? No!"

The air inside the cabin was suddenly too thick to fully inhale.

"You must really think we're stupid," said Bells.

"No, I don't. Not at all. You have it all wrong."

Bells rolled her eyes.

"I have to go," I said, my heart pounding. "I need to talk to Joe."

I paused, one hand pressed against the screen door, the other gripping my notebook. I waited for Hazel, Willa, Shira, or even Bells to tell me to stop. To say my name.

But they didn't.

Not one single voice called out for me to stay.

The walk to Joe's office was a blur. My body was flooded with energy, but I couldn't channel any of it to run. My legs were too shaky. My lungs too tight.

I somehow managed to walk up the four steps to Joe's office and knock on the wooden doorframe.

"Hello, Abby," said Joe, propping the door open with his hip. "What a nice surprise. Everything good, good, good?"

I shook my head. No, no, no.

"You want to come in and talk? Maybe tell me

why you look like you've seen a ghost?" Joe sat down at his desk and motioned for me to sit in the chair on the other side. He folded his hands in his lap, just like he'd done when teaching meditation in the Zendom.

I gripped my notebook, the green fuzz flat under my sweaty palms. "The girls in my cabin think I'm a spy."

"A spy?"

I nodded as tears began to stream from my eyes. "They think I'm going to write about them in a magazine. Or maybe a newspaper. I don't really know. I don't even know how any of that even works."

"I know you don't. Of course you don't."

"I tried to tell them that I'm not famous, but they don't believe me. They hate me."

"Oh man. I'm sure that's not true, Abby. We'll work through this together. I'll help you talk to them. Okay?"

The girls in my cabin would believe Joe,

especially if he explained that my teacher was his sister. But I shook my head.

Because then what? I'd still be a liar. Only admitting the truth to protect myself. They'd never believe that I had been planning to tell them all on my own. They'd never trust anything I said ever again.

Joe brought his index finger to his mouth, his thumb wrapped around his chin. "When my sister first called me about the idea of you coming to Camp Famous, I was apprehensive. We've never had a non-famous camper here before. But you fit right in, Abby. From day one. You might think the other kids like you because you told them you're famous, but that's not what I see. And let me tell you, we've had a lot of famous kids here over the years who the other kids did not like. Being famous doesn't guarantee friendship."

Deep inside I knew Joe was telling the truth. My friends didn't like me because I was famous in the same way I didn't like them because they were famous. I liked Hazel because she was warm and kind. I liked Willa because she was strong and mighty. I liked Shira because she was funny and smart. I liked Bells because she was joyful and silly.

Maybe . . .

"You know," continued Joe, "my sister said she thought that you needed a special boost. But I never saw that in you, Abby. And I mean that in the best, best, *best* possible way."

"A boost?"

"A pick-me-up. A little help. She's always been like that, going out of her way to help people who need her. This one time when we were growing up . . . "

Joe continued on with some story about a neighbor who'd lost a cat. But I was distracted thinking about needing a boost. At first the explanation sounded nice. Like someone lifting me on their shoulders and cheering my name.

But then I realized what it actually meant:

Ms. McIntyre had felt sorry for me. I'd ended up at Camp Famous out of pity.

My favorite teacher, the one who left pencil hearts in the margins of my weekly reflections and always seemed to know what was happening, thought I stood no chance at making friends on my own. In her opinion, my only shot at making friends would be somewhere where the other kids, who were not exactly normal kids, were forced to spend time with me.

The realization was like sliding down a set of stairs. Each bump hurt, but not knowing when my body would stop falling was the scariest part of all. I couldn't handle any more bruises. I was already in too much pain.

"I want to go home."

"Abby, no, no, no. The other kids love you. And you love them. You've always got a smile on your face. You're part of this place. We'll sort out this silly spy thing. It doesn't matter."

"It does. It matters to me. All of it matters."

Joe kneeled by my side. "I can't force you to stay, Abby. But why don't you call home before you make your decision." He moved a phone across the desk. "I'll be waiting right outside the door when you're done."

21

"Grandma?"

"Abby, darling! I'm so thrilled to hear your voice. How are you? How is camp? Tell me everything."

I wanted to tell Grandma everything, but tears swallowed my words. I scrunched the scrap paper with her number in one hand, held the phone to my ear with my other hand, and sobbed. I should have put the phone down to reach for a tissue, or at least moved it aside to wipe my face with my shirt. But I couldn't risk losing Grandma's voice. Her steady *shhh, shhh, shhh, I'm right here, I'm not going anywhere,* was the only thing that kept me breathing.

"Okay, sweetheart," she said when I managed to slow my sobbing. "Tell me the worst part. Just get right to it. We'll fill in the details later."

I thought through all the bad parts. The lying, my cabinmates reading my notebook, the reason Ms. McIntyre arranged this whole thing in the first place.

They were separate, but they all pointed in a similar direction.

"The worst part is that I really, really want to go home."

I'd spent months begging to go to sleepover camp. And now I'd messed up the one thing I wanted most to succeed at—making friends.

I could apologize for lying. I could tell everyone the truth. Joe would back me up.

People would believe me. They might even forgive me. But no matter what, for the next four days, I would be different.

I would be kicked to the outside, trying to look in. Just like at school.

Except at camp there was no escape. No bedroom door to close. No desk to write at. I would have to live in my new reality every second of every single day.

It was too much. I couldn't do it.

"Can you come get me? Please?"

"Abby, no. That won't solve anything. You can't run away from your problems. You have to face them head-on."

"I can't. It's too hard."

"Not for my girl," said Grandma. "You're stronger than this, Abby. I know you are."

"Then why did everyone need to lie to get me here? Mom and Dad. My teacher. Even you lied, Grandma. You acted like I was going to regular camp. You never said a thing about it being a camp for the most famous kids in the world. How come I'm the only one who has to deal with the truth?"

In Grandma's silence I knew that I'd gotten

through to her. She and Mom were different, but when they made up their minds they were similar in their determination.

"Abigail Jane Herman, you are right. I told your parents from the very beginning that their plan was not smart. But they insisted it would be fine. And now they're not here to deal with the consequences. Well, I am. Get me an adult on the phone. I want to speak to someone right now."

I nodded. Put the phone down on Joe's desk. I wiped my eyes with the bottom of my shirt and opened the office door. Joe was sitting right outside, just like he'd promised.

"Joe," I said. "My grandma wants to talk to you."

I could only hear Joe's end of the conversation. But it was enough to understand that there was an airport an hour away and a plane to Florida leaving that evening. Most importantly, that Grandma expected me to be on it.

"Your parents signed a form giving your

grandmother permission to make decisions about your care while they were out of communication," explained Joe when he hung up the phone. "But the final decision is still yours to make, Abby."

Joe waited, hands on his thighs, giving me one last chance to stay. Laughter, shouts, the soft pounding of the tetherball carried through the open windows. Then the dinner bell gonged. Everyone would be heading across the main field to the dining hall.

Maybe Willa was leaping into a series of perfect splits. Maybe Shira was copying her and tumbling to the ground on purpose. Maybe Hazel was running to Shira, hugging her with fake sympathy. Maybe Bells was laughing as she linked one arm through Willa's arm and pulled her into a silly skip.

I saw myself with them, just like always. My arm linked through Bells's other arm. My laughing voice calling out for Hazel and Shira to come on! Catch up! What if they run out of the good desserts!

But that was the other me. The one who

belonged. Not the one who was sitting with tearstained cheeks, the mess of my mistakes filling my belly.

She was not me. I was not her.

It was time for us to part ways.

"Okay," said Joe, reading the answer in my eyes. "Go on and pack up. I'll find Carly and we'll get you out of here before the end of dinner."

As I walked back to Cabin Tranquility, I tried to sharpen my gaze. Clear the blur. This was my last chance to experience camp. To breathe in the evergreen-tinted air. See the shimmer of the sun setting over the lake. Feel the wood chips shift beneath the soles of my flip-flops.

Every second was important. Every view my last.

The hardest was entering Cabin Tranquility. It was technically empty of all my friends, but their presence was still there. A wet towel thrown across Shira's bed. Hazel's tie-dye sweater hanging from a nail. Willa's ballet slippers molded to the shape of her feet. One of Bells's stray socks abandoned beneath the job chart.

I stood, my arms wrapped around my waist, until Carly appeared and I remembered that I didn't have much time.

We began working together to clear my shelves. "Are you sure about this, Abby?" said Carly as she handed me a stack of shirts. "Our cabin won't be the same without you. Camp won't be the same without you."

I dropped the shirts into my navy duffel bag and threw my arms around Carly, just like I'd done to Mom in my bedroom all those months ago when I first learned I was going to sleepover camp. With my squeeze I tried to express that she was the best camp counselor ever and none of this was her fault.

"I'm going to miss you, too," said Carly as she hugged me back. "And you know, I really liked your skit idea. I was excited to see it come to life. It reminded me of how I felt when I was your age. Like every moment was important and also separate. A series of pictures instead of a continuous movie. I replayed everything over and over and over in my head. Examining it like a photograph, I guess. Mostly I was looking for what I could have done better."

I'd never heard peppy, cheery Carly speak like that. Even though I'd suggested the skit idea for an entirely different reason, I related to what she was saying. I had a habit of doing the exact same thing.

The words in my notebook were like pictures. Snapshots. Moments in time. A record of the last few months. Would I ever read my words and not see all the mistakes I'd made? Would the days—at school, at home, at camp—somehow fit together into one single girl?

That seemed impossible.

"Life smoothes out, Abby. Mistakes are hard, but they're not endings. Sometimes they're beginnings." Carly paused, maybe giving me one last chance to change my mind. When I didn't respond, she sighed and said, "I'm going to grab some food before it's all gone. Maybe I'll see you back here next summer?"

I nodded, playing along. The only place I'd ever see anyone from Camp Famous again was on a screen or in a magazine. Except for Oliver, of course.

As Carly left the cabin, there was only one more thing to pack: my notebook.

That fuzzy green cover. Those hot pink sequins. My notebook was the reason I was in this terrible situation. I was tempted to Frisbee it across the cabin. Watch the pages fly and flutter and . . . what?

It was made of paper, not glass. It would land with a thud, not shatter into a million pieces.

And also, my notebook wasn't entirely to blame. Even if I threw it in the lake and watched it sink to a slimy death in the muck at the bottom, what was written between the covers would still be inside of me.

Writing was a relief, but it wasn't a magic wand.

There was no fairy godmother to bibbidi-bobbidi-boo my way out of this.

Besides, now that I'd met a real princess, I realized how much those fairy tales had left out. Bells was complicated. She screamed with joy when we raced unicorns, but her voice dulled when she spoke about her family. She was witty and confident, but she beat herself up over silly mistakes. And when her own feelings were hurt, she hurt other people in turn.

I picked up my notebook and tore out a page. The edges were jagged and messy.

I had something to tell my friend. I didn't have the courage to say it in words. But I could write it down.

Dear Bells,

I'm sorry I lied about being famous. I know you don't believe me, but I really am the most ordinary girl in the world. I've never even had a close friend. But since you can't be famous for being lonely, I pretended to be a writer. I wanted to fit in and be the same as everyone else at camp. I was so tired of feeling different.

I know you'll never forgive me for lying, but I just wanted to say thank you. For the first time ever, I knew how it felt to have a true friend. Even if it was only for a little while.

Abby

I folded the paper in half and slid it under Bells's pillow. The scent of lavender was gone, but her cashmere blanket was just as soft as the day she unpacked it from her trunks. I ran my hand over it one last time.

Then I walked out of Cabin Tranquility and climbed into the front seat of Joe's truck.

I watched until Camp Famous was nothing more than a distant reflection in Joe's side-view mirror.

Two Days Later

The sun in Florida was electric. It burned through the yellow-and-white striped umbrella, the floppy hat on my head, my closed eyelids. No matter how many layers I stacked between me and it, I couldn't find the dark stillness that I craved.

"More sunscreen, sweetheart?" asked Grandma.

I opened my eyes. "No, thanks. I'm going to go for a swim."

"All right. Enjoy yourself."

I pushed myself up from the lounge chair where Grandma and I were sitting beside the pool. The backs of my legs were indented with the chair's plastic slats, but the chlorinated water would puff them right up. This had been my routine for the past two mornings. Chair, pool, chair, pool.

Every time I dove into the water, there was a second when I thought the change of atmosphere would fix something. Not everything. Maybe just some small crack in my shattered life.

But then I would resurface and the same sun would be beating down on my same face. My same brain would replay what had happened at camp, and I would realize there was no glue in the universe strong enough to put me back together.

I was broken. And I always would be.

As I turned to float on my back, Grandma's friend Roger took my abandoned seat under the umbrella. Roger had driven Grandma to the airport to pick me up and knew what had happened at Camp Famous. I'd tried to hold everything in until we arrived at Grandma's apartment, but as Roger drove, with gentle music playing from the radio and Grandma's warm hand clutching mine in the backseat, the story of my time at camp poured out. Every last detail.

So when Grandma began speaking to Roger, checking her phone for details, I knew she was telling him the big news of the day. We'd finally reached my parents. They would arrive in Florida tomorrow morning.

I pushed off the pool wall and floated away from Grandma and Roger. Half of the pool was separated into lap lanes, so it was only a matter of seconds before my head hit a red plastic divider.

I missed the lake. The docks. The beach.

I missed the inflatable unicorns—Majestica, Quantifica, and Bob.

I missed laughter and splashing.

Most of all, I missed my friends.

I wondered what they were doing right now. Maybe they were making bracelets in the Art Hut. Or canoeing. Maybe they were on the docks following along as Cameron Craze taught them his newest dance moves. I pictured Shira trying to copy his fast elbow thrusts, losing her balance, and falling into the water. Last time that happened, we all pretended to tumble in after her.

I laughed at the memory and accidentally sucked chlorinated pool water up my nose. I started to cough.

"Abby, are you okay?" called Grandma, her hands on the armrests of the lounge chair as if she thought she might need to come save me.

I cleared the water and nodded at Grandma. Then I plugged my nose and sank to the bottom of the pool, grateful for the few seconds of quiet.

Grateful that the water hid my tears.

At lunchtime I dried off and joined Roger and Grandma in the retirement village's main dining room. I didn't mind eating with Roger. Company was better than sitting alone underneath Grandma's sympathetic gaze.

After I finished my grilled cheese, Roger pulled

a bag of sour watermelon gummies from under his seat.

"How did you know these were my favorite?" I asked as the sugar coating crunched between my back teeth.

Grandma was a chocolate person. She'd been trying to cheer me up with M&M's and Hershey's bars.

"Wish I could take all the credit," said Roger. "But I had some help. I've got a granddaughter a few years older than you. She's a candy expert, believe it or not. Writes all about it on her computer. I'm told she's very popular. You want to see a picture?"

I shook my head. A popular candy expert was the last thing I wanted to see. She was probably pretty like Hazel. Smart like Shira. Charismatic like Bells. Heck, she was probably even graceful like Willa. Maybe she could toss a gummy bear into the air, spin around on her tiptoes, and catch it in her mouth.

"Well," said Roger. "If you ever want to see a—"

Whirr, whirr, whirr.

A mechanical sound interrupted Roger's words. I assumed it was the tires of an electric wheelchair stalling in the hallway. That happened a lot at the retirement village.

But still, way back in my brain, I couldn't help thinking: *helicopter.* Like the one Joe kept on standby.

I reached for another sour watermelon to keep from crying again.

"Abby! Hey, Abby!"

I could have sworn I heard Shira's voice. Seriously, I had to get a grip.

"Abby, come out here this very instant!"

Bells's voice. Both bossy and bubbly, like giggles were brewing underneath.

I looked at Grandma. Could she tell that I was losing my mind? Should I ask her to slap my cheek and bring me back to reality?

Except Grandma wasn't looking at me. She was helping Roger stand from his seat. They were both staring out at the golf course where a group of kids were running across the grass. Arms pumping. Legs lifting.

There was Bells with her perfect form.

Shira with her loping stride.

Willa with her graceful glide.

Hazel. Kai. And jogging behind all of them, Carly.

All those arms and legs and faces were rushing in my direction!

I pushed back my chair and raced to the double doors that opened onto the golf course. That same electric sun hit my face. But I had no desire to close my eyes against it.

I wanted every second of this to be lit up in full color.

Bells reached me first. She wrapped her arms around me. "Abby," she said. "I found your note, and Joe talked to our whole cabin. I'm so sorry. I never should have looked in your journal, and I never should have doubted you."

CAMP FAMOUS ★

"I never should have lied."

"Two wrongs don't make a right," said Shira, breathless. "It's basic math. Duh."

"Can you forgive us?" said Hazel.

"Please," said Willa. "Camp's not the same without you."

I smiled, unable to answer because every member of Cabin Tranquility wrapped their arms around me. We were swaying side to side, on the cusp of toppling over. It was dark in the center of that group hug, but my heart was lit up with a million sparkles.

When we finally let go of one another, I wiped happy tears from my eyes.

"We would have come sooner, but Joe took some convincing," said Bells. "Something about a violation of privacy. He refused to arrange for transportation, even though this was clearly an emergency situation."

"How'd you change his mind?"

"Bells finally used her one phone call home," said Willa.

Bells shrugged. "It was either plane and helicopter, or the Royal Air Force. Joe made the right decision."

I laughed and hugged Bells again as someone tapped me on the shoulder.

It was Kai. "Hey," he said.

I blushed. Not only because Kai was back in his red hoodie sweatshirt, looking just as pop star cute as when I first saw him at the airport, but because Kai wasn't there when everything fell apart. Which meant that he'd heard about it from my cabinmates, or maybe Joe. What had they told him?

I didn't have it in me to ask.

"You left without saying good-bye," he said.

All I could do was smile, shrug, and hope that Kai understood there was too much to explain with this many people around. "There wasn't time. And also . . . " I shrugged again.

"Yeah," said Kai. "I get it. Sometimes it's hard to know what to say." Now Kai was the one blushing. This was getting awkward.

"That could be a song title for the new album," I joked. "Add it to the list of unknown things."

"Totally," said Kai. "It would fit right in with all the others."

"So you're really writing songs about everything you don't know?"

Kai nodded. He smiled. "Just like I said I would. And I think they're actually good. I can send you some lyrics when I get home if you want."

"Yes," I said. "I'd love to read them."

"Cool," said Kai, fidgeting with the drawstring of his hoodie. "I'll do that."

A crowd had formed at the edge of the golf course. A few residents leaned on canes. Others sat in the outdoor chairs that lined the golf course. Grandma stood with her arms wrapped around her waist, a large smile on her face. Roger was beside her, typing on his phone.

Bells waved with a cupped hand at a woman who was calling her name. I walked over to her and put my hand on her arm, pulling her behind a nearby tree.

"Thanks," said Bells. "I'm not ready to go back to being me."

"Me neither," I said.

Bells smiled. Not her usual whole face smile, but a half one. "Maybe it'll be different now. For both of us."

"What do you mean?"

"Well, we have each other."

"We do?"

"Yep," said Bells. "I'm so happy you're not really a famous writer, Abby. I thought you were hiding your books because you thought I wasn't smart enough to understand them. That's why I got so upset and looked in your notebook."

I remembered how Bells had misspelled *tranquility*. How she needed tutors to get through school. How she turned the pages of her graphic novels super slowly. I hated that my actions made Bells worry like that.

"I would never think that," I said. "I promise. You're so smart, Bells."

"Not about book stuff."

"Well, I'm not smart at friendship stuff. I almost messed everything up."

"You're not the only one."

I paused. "I was going to tell you the truth about not being famous. I swear."

"I believe you," said Bells. "And I really am sorry for looking in your journal. I knew it was private, and I never should have done it. Will you please come back to camp with us?"

"I don't know. . . . "

"But it's cabin skit night tonight. If we leave now, we'll have time to practice combining our ideas."

At the words "cabin skit night," a tiny ball of dread dropped into my stomach. It was one thing to hug it out on the golf course at Grandma's retirement village. It was another thing to go back to camp and face the other campers and counselors.

They would know my story, but they wouldn't

know *me*. I didn't want to stand onstage in front of those judgmental eyes.

"My stuff is already here and my parents are coming tomorrow. I should probably stay."

"But it's our last time all together." Bells glanced at Carly and dropped her voice to a whisper. "We can talk the whole night."

All of us huddled together in bed. A flashlight lighting our faces. Whispered secrets. How could I say no?

Because, I realized, I didn't have to say yes.

The Camp Longatocket website had a testimonial section where campers wrote what they had learned at camp. There were the basic things like how to build a fire, make a dream catcher, flip a kayak. Toward the end of the list was a comment that leaped off my computer screen as if I'd been wearing 3-D glasses. I thought of it as Bells waited for my answer.

I learned that my camp friends will be with me no matter where I go.

Camp was only a few weeks. No matter what. But friendships could last forever. *That* was what I should have been focused on. Making friends I could count on no matter where I was. At camp, at school, or a retirement village in Florida.

I'd done it. I made those friends.

Was it super convenient that they could command helicopters with a single phone call home? Yes. But that wasn't the part that mattered. My friends came to my rescue even though I wasn't perfect, or famous, or anything at all.

They came because they cared about me.

"I think I have to stay," I said.

"Fine. But that means you're coming to visit me this winter."

"Will you send a helicopter?" I joked.

"Of course not," said Bells. "I'll send the royal plane. It's way more comfortable."

Bells and I linked arms and walked back to the group. Now that the initial energy of our reunion had passed, it hit me that everyone was acting differently than at camp.

Kai had his red sweatshirt back on. Hood up, drawstrings dangling. Hazel's hair covered half her face. Willa held her chin at a slight angle, as if someone might ask her to pose for a picture at any second. Bells gave another tight wave with a cupped hand. Only Shira, the U.F.C., was acting like normal.

My friends had left the safety of camp and were back to being their famous selves. And they'd done it for me.

Carly called out a five-minute warning. The helicopter blades began to spin. I could feel Bells's absence in my chest even though she was standing beside me. But I didn't want to start crying, so I focused on the helicopter and said, "I can't believe you all fit inside."

"It seats nine people. So Joe said just your close friends should come."

Bells, Shira, Hazel, Willa, Carly, Kai. Plus the pilot. That was seven people. Even if they were saving a place for my return, that still would have left room for one more person who I wished had come—Oliver.

As the whirl of the helicopter blades blew my hair into my face and muffled my shouts of good-bye, I couldn't help but wonder: Had Oliver not been invited, or had he chosen not to come?

Mom and Dad's arrival was way less dramatic. They pulled up early the next morning in a red rental car. I raced across the parking lot and leaped into Dad's arms. With my legs wrapped around Dad's waist, I leaned over to pull Mom in as well.

Our hug didn't pulse with joy like the hug from my friends. But as my parents held me tight, something inside me broke open. Quiet tears grew to gulping sobs. By the time I lifted my cheek from Mom's shoulder, her shirt was soaked.

"Abby, we missed you so much," said Mom.

"More than you can ever know," said Dad.

"Are you okay, sweetheart?" Mom's eyes moved double time across my face. I couldn't tell if she was looking for signs of change, or maybe seeking forgiveness.

"You should have told me the truth about camp," I said. "I would have been prepared."

"Abby," said Dad. "We didn't want you to prepare."

"We wanted you to be yourself," said Mom. "We didn't expect you to lie."

"You can't have it both ways. You can't lie and expect me to tell the truth. It's not fair."

Dad paused, his lips pressed tight. "You're right," he said. "From now on it's honesty first, deal?" Dad set me down and winced. "Oh, my back. I cannot wait to sleep in a real bed tonight."

"How was your trip?" I asked. I wasn't the only one who'd had an unusual three weeks.

"Fantastic," said Dad. "Except your mom tossed and turned all night, and not just because we were sleeping on the ground. She was so worried about you. If it wasn't for Oliver, she probably would have cut our trip short just in case you needed to reach us."

There was something strangely comforting about the idea of my brave, strong mom tossing and turning with worry. Our worries were different, but we both had them.

Except . . . "What does Oliver have to do with it?"

"I gave Oliver my cell phone number at the airport," said Mom. "Our flight left a few hours after yours, so Oliver called me as soon as you landed at camp. He said you'd already made a friend on the plane and that you were fitting right in."

Oliver's one phone call. He'd used it to call my parents.

I remembered his pinched finger on the plane. His confusion later at lunch when I asked about his injury. Oliver hadn't been in Joe's office getting an ice pack or a Band-Aid. He hadn't hurt his finger at all. Oliver had been faking so he could call Mom without me knowing.

We stayed with Grandma for a few more days. By the time we returned home, I'd stopped replaying my days at Camp Famous over and over in my mind. I still wished I'd done so many things differently. But like knowing about Mom's worries, the fact that I wasn't alone in making mistakes made them easier to bear.

Eventually the fun memories began to replace the hard ones. Especially when group texts from my friends starting pouring into my computer. We communicated half in words, half in emojis. If important things happened—like when we needed to hear about Willa's first day of movie rehearsals or see the packaging for Shira's burping slime— we'd switch to video. Mom or Dad would appear in my doorway and tell me to keep it down. But then they'd lean against my doorframe and smile, trying to listen in. I'd have to shoo them away for some privacy.

I had a separate text chain with Kai. Sometimes he sent me audio clips of his new songs. The lyrics were so catchy. I listened to them over and over.

The only person I couldn't get in touch with was Oliver. I didn't have his number, and every time I went by his house the lights were off and no one answered the door. I even slipped a note through the mail slot asking him to get in touch.

So when my doorbell rang two days before the start of school, I thought maybe it was Oliver and went running to the door.

It was not Oliver. It was Quinn. She stood on my porch, tan and glowing. At first I thought she must have found some new glossy makeup. Then I realized her light sheen was actually sweat.

"Abby," she said. "Tell me this isn't you." Quinn held out her phone, but the screen was locked.

"Um," I said, confused. "What?"

Quinn looked at her phone, realized it was locked, and pressed play on a video. I watched as the screen filled with the sloping green grass of a familiar golf course. My mouth dropped open.

"Hey, sweeties," said a voice from the phone. "It's Candy Queen here to sprinkle some sweetness on your day. This video came from the best grandpa in the whole wide world, my Papa Roger. I'm sure you'll recognize some of these famous faces. They came to surprise a good friend who was having a rough day. Look at this love, guys. Life doesn't get any sweeter than this. I hope it inspires you to spread some good vibes today."

The voice was replaced with music as Bells, Kai, and everyone else from the helicopter came sprinting across the grass. It showed me standing, stunned. The video blurred a little as we hugged, as if the person recording had lowered his or her hand. It cut out entirely after Kai and I started talking.

Papa Roger. Grandma's friend Roger. Whose granddaughter was a popular candy expert. "How did you find this?" I asked.

"Everyone watches Candy Queen. She's the

best. She mostly posts about candy, but sometimes she does these 'spread the sweetness' videos where she shows happy things and whatever. But that's not the point, Abby. The point is . . . " Quinn raised her open hands toward me. "Kai Carter *hugged* you. And so did Princess Isabella Victoria."

I had imagined what kids at school would say if they knew that I'd been to Camp Famous. But I didn't think that they'd actually find out. The photographers at the airport only printed pictures of the most famous kids, like Bells and Kai and Cameron. They never bothered with U.F.C.'s like Shira or Oliver. And since there was no technology allowed at camp, pictures never leaked.

Part of me wanted to brag about all my new friends. Okay, more than brag. I wanted to stand in the school hallway and shout about it as loudly as I could.

But I worried about what would follow: The eye rolls. The doubt. The rumors that I was a show-off liar.

Here was actual proof of my new friendships in the hands of one of the most popular girls in my grade. So why did part of me want to delete the video from Quinn's phone?

"I met them this summer," I said.

"Where? Where did you go to meet Kai Carter? TELL ME NOW!"

As Quinn leaned toward me, hunger for information in her bulging eyes, I thought about that testimonial on the Camp Longatocket website.

My camp friends are with me no matter where I go.

I squared my shoulders like Willa.

I thought fast like Shira.

I called up my inner confidence like Bells.

I smiled like Hazel.

But I spoke in my own words: "Sorry, Quinn. Kai's busy rehearsing for his tour, but I'll tell him you're a big fan."

Then I slammed the door shut.

The first day of sixth grade. New building. New teachers. New kids.

"You ready for this?" asked Dad. "Middle school. I can't believe it."

I was too nervous to answer. I unbuckled my seat belt and slid out of the car. Normally I would take the bus. Dad only drove me because it was the first day. Mom had offered to reschedule her first meeting and come with us, but I'd had all the pep talks I could take.

Unlike Mom, Dad understood that this was not

the time for deep conversations or, worst of all, a good-luck kiss.

I put my backpack over one shoulder as Dad's car was swept away in the rapidly moving drop-off line. I'd been in the middle school building before. Last year, in fifth grade, we'd taken a tour as a class. We'd walked in a single-file line, shuffling awkwardly as we tried to take everything in without banging into the person in front of us.

Now there was no line, just a random spread of kids. It was up to me to decide which way to move.

Quinn stood in a tight bunch with her normal group of friends, with one exception. Marin was a few feet away. When Quinn had come to my door without Marin, I'd assumed that Marin had been busy, or maybe on vacation with her family. Now I wondered if something had happened between them over the summer.

I was so used to Marin and Quinn sticking side by side, their friendship the ultimate sign of their strength. Standing apart they just looked like nervous sixth graders. Quinn flipped her hair. Marin wrapped the strap of her backpack around her finger.

I was still drawn to them. Maybe I always would be. But instead of feeling desperate, I was simply curious about what had happened between them.

"Abby," said a voice at my side. "Hello. How have you been?"

I would recognize that voice anywhere. Formal and stiff, with a bit of a squeak. And also, a lot of kindness. Oliver Frank! Finally!

"Oliver, where have you been? I made my mom drive by your house a hundred million times."

"There was a technology retreat that I had to cover for work and then my family went on vacation. I only returned home yesterday. Thankfully the lectures were enormously enlightening. Did you know—"

"Oh," I said, cutting Oliver off before he went on to describe what exactly was so enlightening. There was something important I'd been waiting to tell him. "I'm sorry for leaving camp without saying good-bye. I was really embarrassed about everything."

"You didn't need to be."

"That's not how it felt at the time. I didn't think I could face it."

Oliver tilted his face toward the sky. He was trying to understand, but he would never really get it. Oliver was comfortable with himself in a way that I was just starting to be.

Before Camp Famous, I'd thought Oliver's comfort stemmed from being a little out of it. Now I knew it came from how he felt inside, not that he missed what was going on around him on the outside.

It also helped that Oliver had a whole other life. Everyone needed a break from being themselves for a bit. When being Oliver Frank became too dull or maybe lonely, he could step into the role of Francis Oliver. When being famous became too invasive, the kids at camp could spend three weeks in privacy.

What was I supposed to do when things got

hard? When the enormous middle school building rose in front of me and kids began to gather in groups to walk up the front steps together? I still hadn't figured that out.

I knew what *not* to do. Lying, faking, pretending to be somebody different was not the answer. And neither was trying to deal with it on my own.

"Oliver," I said. "Do you think we'll be in any of the same classes?"

"I hope so, Abby. That would be nice."

"Yeah, it would be."

Oliver and I walked together, side by side, toward the school building.

Quinn called out to me. "Hey, Abby. I'm so excited to see you. Did you read that Kai Carter's tour is coming here soon? I thought maybe we could all go as one big group?" She looked back at her waiting friends. "Do you think you can get us backstage passes?"

Oliver raised one eyebrow. Quinn had looked right past him as if he didn't exist.

"Oh," I said. "I can't. I'm going with Oliver. But maybe we'll see you there."

I pulled Oliver forward, away from Quinn and her confused stare.

"I would love to attend Kai's concert with you, Abby," said Oliver. "That sounds like a lot of fun. Maybe Kai wants to come over for dinner before he goes onstage. I'll text him after school."

"Perfect," I said. "We can make cupcakes with gummy bears on top for dessert, just like at camp."

"Just like at camp."

Oliver and I walked into the middle school building. We were in separate homerooms, but we made a plan to meet up for lunch. I found my locker halfway down a long hall. Marin opened the locker next to mine.

"Oh my gosh, Abby," she said. "We're locker neighbors. I'm so glad."

"You are?"

"Totally. I was so worried all summer long about my locker and who I would be next to. Stupid, right? I mean, it's just a locker. But the school tells us who's in our homeroom, so I knew I didn't have to worry about that. I just—"

Marin paused. She looked over her shoulder, even though no one could hear us over the metallic banging of the locker doors.

"Quinn and I had a big fight this summer," continued Marin. "She hates me and she turned everyone against me. Which isn't that surprising. We were growing apart for a while. Quinn's just not very . . . nice, you know? So I'm on my own, I guess. Time to make some new friends!"

Marin spoke with fake cheer. She was clearly nervous. I was so shocked that Marin—pretty, nice, popular Marin—was worried about making friends that I forgot about my backpack resting on the edge of my open locker.

When I took a step forward to make room for everyone walking by, the backpack fell to the ground and landed on its side. None of my books fell out. But when I bent down to pick it up, a tiny pink object rolled out from the open front pocket.

Wilbur! The adorable pig eraser with the curlicue tail that Marin had given to me last year. In all the excitement of camp, I'd forgotten that I'd packed him in my backpack along with my notebook. Poor little guy. He had been trapped in there all summer.

Or maybe, he'd been hiding all summer. Waiting for the perfect time to reappear.

I handed Wilbur to Marin. "You probably don't remember," I said. "But you gave this eraser to me last year when I was having a bad day. I think he's good luck. Why don't you take him today?"

Marin placed Wilbur upright in her open palm. "Of course I remember. He's so cute. Are you sure? I don't want to take him from you if he's good luck."

"I'm sure," I said. "I want you to have him."

"Wow. Thanks so much. So I'll see you back here after first period? I'll report on anything lucky that happens. Like maybe not running into you-know-who!"

I smiled. "I'll meet you right here."

"And Abby," called Marin. "Maybe you can take him with you to second period. You know, for good luck."

"Yeah," I said. "That sounds great. I need all the luck I can get."

"It's middle school," said Marin. "I bet we'll be passing him back and forth all year long."

That night I pulled my green notebook out of my desk drawer. I hadn't opened the pages since getting home from camp, but I had thought about them. *A lot.*

When I'd organized my desk to prepare for the start of school, I could hear the notebook whispering to me through the wooden barrier of the drawer.

It said: *Open me.*

It said: *Remember me.*

It said: *You're different now. You've changed.*

It said: *It will be okay.*

But had I? Would it? How could I know?

I looked at the bare wall above my bed. The space where I'd imagined hanging the Cabin Tranquility plaque with all our names signed in paint. Hazel had told us that she'd found the cabin plaque in her luggage. Hazel hid the plaque in the back of her closet so her mom would never find it. She wanted to keep camp private.

Hazel hoped that we weren't mad about the plaque being in a dark hiding spot, and we all promised that we understood. Hazel wasn't ready to stand up to her mom yet. But she would be someday. The strength was growing inside her. It was only a matter of time.

There was something growing inside me, too. I'd felt it that morning when I walked into school with Oliver. And when I handed Wilbur to Marin. For so long I'd convinced myself that I needed an invitation to move from the outside of a group to the inside. Maybe I'd had it backward.

Maybe I could make my own inside and invite other people to join me. I could walk through the doors of school first, without watching to see how other kids did it, even if I didn't know what was waiting for me inside.

I had a video call scheduled that weekend with my camp friends. I'd promised to tell them every single detail of middle school.

But that night it was just me. Alone. I pressed my palm against all those hot pink sequins. I ran my fingertip over the fuzzy green cover.

I opened to a blank page and began to write.

Acknowledgments

An enormous thank you to my writing dream team: my editor, Martha Mihalick, and my agent, Alex Slater.

Thank you to everyone at Greenwillow Books: Virginia Duncan, Tim Smith, Sylvie Le Floc'h, and the entire marketing, publicity, library, and sales teams for working so hard to get books into the hands of young readers.

Thank you to Maeve Norton for this stunning cover.

And to my family: Jeff, Ella, Liv, and Aven. You are the heart of everything I write.